The Quilt Ripper

Mary Devlin Lynch
and
Debbie Devlin Zook

© 2015 Mary Devlin Lynch/Debbie Devlin Zook
All rights reserved
Published by *DevlinsBooks*

ISBN No. 978-0692616611

Everyone we know thinks they have a book inside them, waiting to get out. And they're probably right. Writing it is the easy part; releasing it for other people to read, ah, there's the rub! But you have to find a way to trust that the stories you tell will be appreciated by those who read them. You may be surprised to find that other people get it, more of them than you ever dreamed.

Prologue

HANNAH HADDON – July 1759, London

Hannah carefully wrapped the last of the new shirts for Henry and tucked it into the top of her oaken trunk. She settled herself on the divan, blotted her warm face with a perfumed handkerchief, and pushed the locks of damp red curls off her neck. She glanced longingly at the closed window. But the foul air outside was much worse than the warm air inside.

She picked up her silk fan and fanned herself for a minute. When she felt slightly refreshed, she finished her job. She gave the wrapped shirt one last pat for luck, closed the trunk and locked it. The click of the clasp on the lock made all the changes in her life suddenly more real. Say goodbye to the life you know in England; sail off to a new world with only what you could pack or carry.

She went to her writing desk and took up the quill. What could she say to Henry? He had been in the colonies for six months now. She missed him. He knew that. London was a cesspool in the summer, the filth in the streets heated to an almost unbearable stench. He knew that, too. She wanted nothing more than to join him in a place where they could breathe fresh air. That he also knew, only too well. He was risking everything to make that happen.

Hannah wanted to believe all would be well but just now she felt scared and lonely. She closed her eyes for a minute and brought Henry to her: envisioned his warm brown eyes and his smile, tried to capture the feel of his strong arms around her.

She took a deep breath and stroked the black ink across the paper.

My dearest, I entrust this letter and the oaken trunk to Cynthia Stanton, whom you will remember, I am sure.

I confess to wishing I were boarding the Walston *in her place. Your cousin, Joshua, has promised to arrive no later than August 1st to take over the keeping of the house. Hence, I have obtained passage on the* Ajax *under Captain Reilly Jones on August 5th. Guard this trunk, my love, as it contains items which will be* precious *to us in our new lives. James is coming with me still; perhaps my wayward brother will finally take a wife in this new place!*

I count the days, my love. ℋ

She signed it with her big H and the flourish that always made him laugh. She looked at the note and hoped he would pay attention to the word "precious." Rumors had abounded in their circle of jewel trunks and purses disappearing en route to the colonies. Those items not plundered by a bold ship's crew disappeared during inspections by unscrupulous customs officials. Her enterprising cousin, Agatha, had secreted her "precious" items within her clothing and linens and they had arrived intact.

Hannah had laughed when she was told the story but then realized how practical an idea it truly was. She had so little to begin with: her mother's pearls and diamond bracelet, a gold ring from her great-grandmother, and lovely sapphire earrings that were a wedding gift from her uncle. She had

2

accepted that she would have to exchange them for household necessities in her new place. But even knowing she would have to part with them at some point, it was still hard for her to let them out of her sight.

Hiding valuables in textiles was smart but Hannah had added another innovation of her own. Her trunk was constructed with a secret hollow in the support boards of the back. It slid apart like a Chinese puzzle and she had carefully tucked several small purses of pounds and guineas that they could ill afford to lose into the hidden space.

Her note completed, she rose and laid a hand in benediction on her trunk with a silent prayer for its safe arrival in the colonies. Her reverie was interrupted by the arrival of her friend. Cynthia flounced in ahead of her uncle and two servants.

"My darling Hannah!"

Hannah smiled at her dramatic entrance. Cynthia liked to put on airs well beyond her twenty years but Hannah knew that a loyal and kind heart beat beneath her daringly revealing dress bodice. "Cynthia! Thank you again for ..."

Cynthia waved a gloved hand. "It's nothing, truly." She giggled. "As I'm going to Aunt Louisa's house, I have no household goods of my own to transport. Having your trunk makes me feel more ... substantial somehow."

Her Uncle John, who had entered quietly and stood patiently behind her, shook his head.

Hannah took both her friend's hands. "You will take good care, won't you?" She had a sudden sense of foreboding and found herself reluctant to part with the bubbly girl.

Cynthia pouted and slapped her fan against Hannah's arm. "Don't you even think about putting a damper on my great adventure, you dreadful woman."

3

Her uncle waved his men toward the trunk and they secured the straps, doffed their caps, and departed, lugging the heavy piece between them.

Hannah stopped Cynthia's uncle as he turned to follow.

"Dear Mr. Stanton, safe journey to you," she said quietly.

He humored her with a smile and a nod. The males of his house were as taciturn as the females were talkative and sociable. His quiet composure seemed to reflect his trade in the silent solidity of the written word; he dealt primarily in books.

John Stanton had already established a household in the colonies and settled his wife, Cynthia's Aunt Louisa, in Boston. During his absence, Cynthia had stayed with a cousin in the country west of London. Of course, she hated it (boring!), and waited impatiently for her chance to venture forth into a new land.

But it was only when he was assured of their place in the new world would her uncle consent to escort her. Cynthia had become his ward several years ago, his only brother's only child, and he did his best to protect and restrain the boisterous impulsive little creature. She was his only heir and the future of the Stanton family, for better or worse.

"Well, my dear, off we go," Cynthia said boldly but Hannah heard the faintest tremor in her voice.

Suddenly, Hannah wanted to share the secret of her trunk with Cynthia. But she fought off that urge. It would only add weight to the poor girl's already unsettled and excited state. Besides, she would surely tell her uncle. Agatha had said emphatically that only one person could keep a secret. So Hannah bit her tongue.

"Well, here is the key for the trunk, please keep it safe and give it to Henry when you arrive." She handed Cynthia a blue velvet ribbon with a key tied on the end. "And tell

Henry …," then she remembered the note and grabbed the envelope from her desk. "Please give him this, won't you?"

"Certainly, but we shall all be looking for you just a few weeks hence."

"Goodbye, my sweet Cynthia." She hugged her and Cynthia kissed her cheek fondly and then was gone.

She was at her bedroom window the next morning, watching the ship being loaded at the dock down the hill. She saw her big trunk going onboard and her stomach jolted. She had done her best; even if the crew went through it, all they would find was clothing and bedding. When Cynthia's carriage appeared, she opened the window, ignoring the stench, and waved. As if she could sense Hannah's presence, the pretty blonde in bright blue turned and waved back. Hannah blew her a kiss before she closed the window.

A little devil whispered in her ear that Cynthia was perhaps overly fond of Henry, and there she was, on her way to him before Hannah could take her place as his wife in their new home.

Unlike Hannah, she was free to go. As a young, single woman, Cynthia didn't have Hannah's responsibilities for securing the house now that Henry had truly decided to move to the colonies permanently. Hannah scolded herself for such unkind thoughts. She was being ridiculous; Cynthia was her friend and she trusted Henry's love.

Nevertheless, as she watched the ship until it was out of sight, she felt very alone.

Chapter One

Tink! Tink! Tink! Queenie McQuinn tapped the water glass in front of her with the end of her pen. "Your attention, please. The weekly meeting of Cutler Quilting Guild Number One will now come to order."

Queenie's very formal call to order always elicits a giggle from the group because, as far as we know, there is no Quilting Guild Number Two in our small town of Cutler, Pennsylvania. We stifled our chatter to pay attention.

This meeting was a special one to all of us because it was our week to work on charity projects. We make items and then donate them for sale to raise money for needs within our community.

We are a mixed group of quilters. Three of us have jobs: Queenie is our guild president, a master quilter, and the owner of Queenie's Quilt Shop (the only quilting store in town); Judy Smythin works as a cashier at Miller's Drugstore; and I, Miranda Hathaway, am the town librarian. Brittany Bartlett is a stay-at-home mom; twins Sarah and Harriet Moore are retired teachers; and our newest member, Gabe Downing, well, we're not sure how to categorize Gabe. He's our man of mystery. He seems to suggest that he's retired, but he's only been with us a couple of weeks so we haven't wormed his entire life story out of him yet. Trust me on this, we will.

"I want to begin by thanking each of you for coming to help with our charity project today." Queenie starts each of these special meetings exactly the same way.

At our other meetings, we work on our own projects and help each other with fabric selections, quilt patterns, etc. We also try to solve the problems of the world, our town, and each other while we stitch and sew.

"I'm sure you have all noticed that Gabe is absent." Queenie paused for dramatic effect before continuing.

"He called to say he had business out of town but will be back next week."

After another theatrical pause, and a look through her glasses at a note, she added, "Today, we'll be making simple nine-patch pillows to be sold at a craft fair at the high school in two weeks. You all know the Seth Lowry family had a fire recently. It looks like it will be several months before they can get back into their home, so they could use some help with the costs of their temporary housing, food, clothes, and such. We all know what dealing with insurance companies can be like." A murmur of assent assured her that we did.

Queenie checked another note. "There will also be a bake sale for them at the firehouse next Saturday morning in case you want to help with that, too. I plan on taking some things over and I'll be glad to pick up yours as well. Just let me know."

Queenie's voice was rich and deep. She spoke slowly, drawing out each syllable and word.

Her real name's not Queenie, of course, it's Elizabeth, but she's been called Queenie all her life. If you wonder whether the name came first or the attitude, wonder no more. According to her dad, who passed a few years ago, the baby girl had an attitude from day one, demanding to be the center of attention and considering all that was given to her simply her due, so her father nicknamed her his "little queenie" and it stuck.

The *little* went by the wayside long ago. Queenie's a tall, large-framed woman, with a pile of orange-red hair and pale blue eyes. Her magnifying glasses, hanging on a silver chain

7

with colored crystal beads interspersed in it, are always at the ready, balanced precariously on her ample bosom. Her wardrobe tends to long, brightly colored tunics with pockets, worn with straight-leg black pants or tights. The pockets often bulge with measuring tape, pins, and thread. Today's top was sunflower yellow and her earrings were large sunflower buttons to match.

Queenie was "in the theater" in her earlier years. She performed in college and in the local community theater until the good roles became harder and harder to find for, to put it kindly, a woman of a certain age.

So she turned her hand to the skills she'd been taught by her mother and grandmother. She opened her quilt shop and began to turn out beautifully designed quilts and sell the fabrics and notions needed to create all kinds of masterpieces of needlecraft.

Yet she never quite left acting behind her, grafting her booming stage voice and grand gestures onto her everyday persona. When it was suggested she teach classes, she welcomed the chance to command a room again and, eventually, the guild was formed. One thing for sure, Queenie knows how to make the most of a moment.

"Now, ladies, let's get to work." She clapped her hands enthusiastically. "We're doing our simple nine-patch pillows. I believe everyone has their assignments."

Precut strips of fabric lay next to two machines. I sat down at one and Queenie took the other. Or, to be more specific, I took the one that wasn't powder blue and, therefore, always hers. It was easy work to sew three strips together. I alternated colors: dark, light, dark; while she did the opposite mix: light, dark, light.

We flipped the completed three-strip pieces to Brittany, who was seated at a cutting table right in front of the sewing machines. She used a large ruler and rotary cutter to cut them into three-block strips. Then she alternated the strips and pinned them together. She tossed them to Judy, who used the third sewing machine to sew them into the nine-patch blocks. She added the precut backing fabric squares and then stitched the front and back together, leaving an opening for turning.

Judy then tossed each one to Sarah. Sarah and Harriet were sitting on stools at another cutting table with bags of polyester fiberfill in front of them. Their job was to stuff each pillow and hand stitch the opening shut, with an exposed tag proudly proclaiming it a product of the Cutler Quilt Guild. We liked to think that our community valued our work and would pay a better price for guild goods.

Once Queenie and I were ahead of the others, she would switch to sewing fronts to backs with Judy. We were a mini factory assembly line.

We worked in silence, each absorbed in our own thoughts. Since I was sewing short straight seams, not much concentration was needed and my thoughts wandered. I was soon thinking contentedly how happy I was to be here.

A couple of years ago, this space had been deserted and boarded up, like much of our dying downtown area. Main Street vendors were driven out of business or had relocated to the shopping mall about three miles away. Thankfully, the town council woke up and started to work at saving it, offering building owners rent subsidies and tax breaks to attract new small businesses like Queenie's, even scheduling events like "Support Local Businesses Day."

Residents are encouraged to shop the downtown through specials and coupons in the local papers. Parking spaces are also free, compliments of the newly formed Chamber of Commerce. It's heartening how much revitalization there has

9

been and I'm happy to say that currently there isn't a vacant storefront in the three-block downtown area.

Like most small towns, our kids are going off to school and not coming back, but our population holds steady at about 3,000. It may sound selfish, but the locals (including me) simply want the town to keep being home. And most of us are committed to supporting shops like Queenie's or The Grapes of Grath, a wine shop owned by my new friend, Vinnie Grath.

Back to work, you! I pulled my attention back to Queenie's. I love Queenie's shop and, if I'm not at home or at work, you'll often find me here. Without looking up, I was aware of the fabrics in the sales room that takes up most of the space in the shop. The big open space has floor-to-ceiling shelves of fabrics in every color you can imagine. They form two L-shapes along the walls on both sides and turn toward the arched opening to the workroom at the back.

A bay window in the front provides a display area with constantly changing exhibits, usually items made by Queenie or her customers. Sometimes these quilts or wall hangings are for sale; sometimes they are vintage items on loan for display only. There's always something lovely and colorful to entice street traffic to come inside.

If the workroom, the storage room, bathroom, and Queenie's office were all put together, they'd probably be about the same size as the sales room.

On the left side, toward the center of the room, a row of cabinets containing threads of every color and needles of all sizes form an aisle. On the right, three sewing machines are set up a few feet away from the fabric shelves. In the middle of the shop are three large cutting tables for measuring out customers' fabric purchases. We sit around one of them on tall stools for our meetings. A checkout counter with cash register sits just inside the front door.

The ceiling is lined with rows of true-color lighting fixtures that help distinguish shades for selecting fabric. The black-and-white checkerboard tile floor makes it easy to sweep up bits of fabric and thread at the end of the day.

The workroom is all about hand quilting hoops hanging on the wall and larger quilting frames standing on the floor. Usually one frame holds an ongoing project that Queenie and her friends work on several times a week.

Did I mention that everything is blue? The walls, the paper supplies, including the shopping bags, are all Queenie's favorite color. My eyes had drifted to the stack of pale blue shopping bags on the front counter, all with the bold *Queenie's* logo in gold (and, yes, there's a crown over the 'i' where the dot should be). I smiled to myself.

I know that Queenie's larger-than-life personality isn't for everyone but not everyone knows she has a heart as big as her hair. The idea of doing charity work once a month was hers, and I know that as busy as she is with the shop, teaching, and the guild, she volunteers one day a week at the local soup kitchen. She puts me to shame. I could do better at giving back to the community that I grew up in and love.

Chapter Two

My daydreaming was interrupted by a loud outburst. "Ohmigod! What a bitch!"

The machines stopped dead and all heads turned toward the speaker. Brittany is a tiny pixie of a girl, with dark brown hair and eyes, who is, impossibly, the mother of two preschoolers. Jackson is four and Samantha is about to turn three. As she herself admits, she has quite a mouth on her for the mother of small children. She once confessed that she came from a family of five, the other four being older brothers and, given her size, she had to scream to be heard. Old habits die hard.

She sure had my attention. "Hey, what's going on over there?"

Judy's face flushed. "Sorry, Miranda! I was just telling Brit about Susan Duncan."

"That bitch went into the drugstore and screamed at Judy! Can you believe the nerve?" Brittany was puffed up like a little bantam hen.

"Susan Duncan?" No, I couldn't believe it. "That doesn't make any sense. She's so quiet! What on earth happened?"

Judy cleared her throat and addressed her rapt audience. "I was at the cash register checking out Mrs. Marshall and Susan marched up and started shouting at me. Poor Mrs. Marshall, you know she's 89 years old, was all upset."

There were nods of understanding. Everyone in town knew Mrs. Marshall and treated her with care and respect as she determinedly continued to do her own errands around town.

"I walked her out to the car, like I always do, and explained to Jim—you all know her son who has the insurance agency—what had happened."

We all nodded in unison. The old dear had three sons and they took turns caring for her.

"Well, I was so embarrassed."

"So Susan was still there when you went back inside?" Even after having acquired some patience with Queenie's dramatic performances, I was curious to get to the cause of such an unusual confrontation.

"Oh no, she followed me right outside! As soon as I closed that car door, she lit into me again."

"What on earth was her problem?" Queenie demanded.

"She said that Aiden was supposed to be the starting pitcher on the Cutler High baseball team this year and Tommy took it away from him." Judy's motherly indignation raised her voice slightly.

"I know he's my son and all but that kid's worked really hard. He and his dad have been throwing a baseball back and forth in our yard for hours at a time since he was six."

"So this whole damn scene was because her son doesn't get to be the starting pitcher on the high school baseball team?" Brittany piped up.

Judy flushed slightly at Brittany's language. "Yes, but even worse, the coach moved Aiden to the outfield. She was ranting that all he's ever wanted to be was a pitcher and now he's stuck in right field. She said he was completely devastated." She added drily, "And apparently, so is his mother."

"Even so, that's no excuse for her to confront *you*, especially at your workplace. That's really over the top," I commented.

"Oh, there's more, Miranda!" Judy huffed. "She said the only reason Tommy got to be the starter is because Tom and Coach Confer played ball together when they were in school and are still friends."

Harriet spoke up. "Well, I never would have expected this from little Susie Mayer! She was the sweetest child in school. We both had her in class." She glanced at her sister who gave a confirming nod. "Very quiet, loved to read, and never caused any problems. This is just so ..."

"... upsetting." Sarah shook her head.

"That's awful."

"Hard to believe."

The supportive comments echoed around the group.

"What on earth did you do?" I asked.

Judy, bolstered by the support of the group, squared her shoulders. "I tried to get her to calm down. I asked if she had time to get a cup of coffee with me down at Sylvia's so we could talk, but she said she had to get home."

She paused. "Of course, as soon as Tommy got home from school, I talked to him. He and Aiden have been friends since elementary school, and some things are more important than a starting position."

Brittany gestured with a brisk hand wave for Susan to get on with it. "So what did he say?"

"This is where it gets truly weird. Tommy said that he and Aiden are still friends and they're both fine with it. When I told him that Susan is upset and said Aiden was really upset, too, Tommy said that just isn't true."

"Weirder and weirder," Brittany muttered.

"I know, and get this! Tommy said Aiden went to the coach and asked to be moved to the outfield. He said that he didn't think he was good enough to be starting pitcher. He wanted more playing time, which he'll get as a fielder, and he's a really good hitter, so he thinks he can drive in runs for the team. The kid thought he was doing what was best for him and for the team!"

It made sense to me. "Apparently, Aiden needs to let his mom know how he feels, and that this switch was his idea."

"Let's all bear in mind that Susan's husband died only about a year ago." Harriet's plump face saddened. "Aaron wasn't even 40 years old, and to have a sudden massive heart attack like that? We had him in school, too. I'm sure it's been hard for her to lose him that way." She turned toward Sarah who added, "Very hard."

Queenie had been listening quietly to this conversation but now her rich voice summed up what we were all thinking. "You have to clear the air, Judy." She waved a brightly beringed hand. "You and Tommy should go over there and have a talk with her and Aiden. That way everybody can move on with no hard feelings."

Judy's face brightened. "You're right. The direct approach, I like it. Thanks, everyone!"

We went back to work and everyone appeared to feel better, except Brittany. I could tell she was still fuming. Our little pepper pot! It was sweet that she was so defensive of Judy but it also crossed my mind that spending time with the older, wiser women of our group was good for her. She had a little maturing to do. Well, maybe more than a little.

Since the shop is open for business on Saturday afternoons when we meet, people like to stop by to see what we're working on. While we appreciate their support and enthusiasm, it can slow us down. Most Saturdays, when we're working on our own projects, we love to stop and chat, but on charity days we value uninterrupted work time.

Today was a good one. We made great progress with only two quick drop-in visitors late in the afternoon. Mrs. Grant came by to get more pink thread for her new granddaughter's quilt and to show us baby Lily's photos on grandma's cellphone. After we enthusiastically admired the little one, she left with a big smile just as Andy walked in. He held the door for her and she kept smiling and nodded as she passed.

Andy showed up in town about six months ago. His camo pants, army jacket, and heavy boots told us he was likely a vet; his unwillingness to talk with people pointed to PTSD (Post-traumatic Stress Disorder). The local army recruiter, Herb Norwood, has had some long talks with him. I'd guess most of the talking was done by Herb, because I've never heard Andy speak more than a few words at any given time.

I know more about it than most folks here in town. Herb was one of my husband Harry's best friends. He's the one who came to the house to get me after the hunting accident. Herb keeps in touch with me and, in one of his visits, he told me about Andy, in total confidence of course.

Using the basics of name, rank, and serial number, Herb had identified our Andy as Andrew Perretta from Philadelphia and he was married. Herb tracked down his wife and gave her a call. The man choked up as he told me about his painful conversation with her.

Maria Perretta was so relieved to know Andy was safe that she burst into tears on the phone. Bit by bit, she pulled herself together and shared his story with Herb. Andy was a staff sergeant in the Army and served tours in Iraq and Afghanistan. He'd commanded several different squads of soldiers, many of whom hadn't made it back. He was wounded when a landmine destroyed the transport he was traveling in with three of his men. The others had been killed. Andy received serious injuries to his legs and was sent to Bethesda Hospital for surgery followed by months of rehabilitation. When he was discharged and sent home, he'd tried to adapt to his old life but suffered terrible headaches and nightmares. His physical wounds were healing but not his emotional ones. She had tried to be patient with him.

She woke up one morning to find a note on the kitchen counter saying:

> *Maria,*
> *I love you. Never doubt that. I need some*
> *time and space. Please try to understand.*

Maria was distraught. The only things he took with him were his duffle bag and fatigues. She wasn't even sure if he had any money. Her first instinct was to go looking for him. She cried, she screamed. She read his note again and again until she realized that the note held more words than he had spoken at one time since he'd returned to the States. It gave her hope that he'd eventually work through the physical and emotional trauma. She had spoken to an Army psychiatrist who recommended that they leave him alone for the time being. So Maria made the very hard decision to let him go.

Somehow, he traveled about 150 miles to end up in Cutler.

Maria gave Herb the name and number of the Army psychiatrist who was familiar with Andy's case and they were in touch. He was giving Herb some helpful hints in dealing with Andy's PTSD.

Knowing all this, I find myself watching for signs of improvement that might signal that Andy is getting closer to going home to the wife who is waiting for him. He does seem to be more relaxed as he wanders around town now. I think he knows this is a safe place and he's been adopted by

17

most of the locals. But it still feels like he has a long way to go.

He seems to have a special fondness for Queenie's, yet he only comes into the shop when our group is working. I don't understand why but I assign it to not wanting to scare away Queenie's customers. It's true he's a little rough-looking around the edges and a few of our older ladies might be intimidated by him.

Even though he showers down at the Y or at the church rectory where they have set aside a room for him, he usually needs a shave. The local Thrift Shop has a sign posted that reads: "All clothing free to veterans. As you have served us, let us now serve you." They put the sign up shortly after Andy came to town and Herb brought him in the first time to get him familiar with the shop. They also receive packs of new t-shirts and underwear that are donated specifically for Andy. So when he comes in they fill a bag and toss in the underwear as well.

And we make sure he doesn't go hungry. There's not a place in town where he's not welcome. Most of the restaurants, like Sylvia's Diner, have a cup set aside where folks can throw in their change or more for Andy's meals. He spends hours sitting in a chair watching TV at the local furniture store. The owner often brings him a sandwich and soda and joins him for lunch.

At any rate, we all greeted him, but quietly. He didn't startle as easily as he used to but we all knew he would leave if it got too loud. He sat down at a cutting table. Brittany brought him a bottle of water from the workroom refrigerator when she went to get one for herself. He nodded as he picked it up and took a long drink. A slight smile appeared and disappeared quickly on his face. We let him sit there quietly as we cranked out the work.

Finally, Queenie stopped sewing and said, "Okay, ladies! Sarah and Harriet please finish up what you've got there and we'll call it a day. Great work!" She nodded at the pile of pillows stacked on the cutting table in front of Andy.

"I'll get some big boxes and the rest of you can help me pack them up before you go."

After I'd put one or two pillows in a box, I looked up as Andy handed me another one to put in. I said, "Thank you, Andy."

He picked up another one and handed it to me. I knew the other women were sneaking looks at us and I knew they were surprised as I was but everyone kept packing up without comment so they wouldn't scare him away.

"I'll let Loretta Pace know they're ready to be picked up. She's in charge of the craft sale. Thank you all for coming. See ya next Saturday!" Queenie dismissed us cheerfully.

As I was walking to my car, Andy fell into place beside me. "Stranger in town." He said while shaking his head slightly. "Up to no good."

"Okay, thanks." I had no idea what that was supposed to mean. At my car, I turned and said, "See ya, Andy. You take care now." He continued walking down the street, silent again.

I was driving by Sylvia's Diner and decided to stop to pick up some supper. *I deserve it. I've worked hard today.*

As I waited for my order, I pondered. What on earth was Andy talking about? It was more words than I'd ever heard him speak. I've heard him whisper, "thank you," a couple of times, but this was very specific. At that moment, I was hungry and too tired to think clearly. Oh well, he'd spoken to me directly and that was a step forward.

Sylvia came from the kitchen carrying a brown bag. "That'll be $8.95 for the meatloaf dinner to go, Miranda." She set my dinner on the counter.

"Thanks, Sylvia." I handed her $20 and nodded toward the collection cup for Andy's meals. "Put the rest in there, will ya?"

She smiled. "Will do! Thanks, hon, see ya later."

Chapter Three

Gabe had missed the Saturday Quilt Guild gathering because he was, indeed, out of town on business. But he hadn't planned to be.

Earlier that week, Thursday, in fact, he had been sitting at the small kitchen table in his Cutler apartment above the wine shop, writing up the few notes he had on his current active case. When his cellphone beeped, the number surprised him. It had only been two months since he'd escorted Macy McMillan back to school after spring break. By his calendar she should be there at least another month until summer break.

"Gabe Downing."

"This is Peter McMillan. I have a job for you."

"I'm working another case right now so it depends on what you need."

"I need you to fly to Paris and find out what's going on with my kid."

"I see." Gabe had found out a long time ago that silence was an effective tool to get information out of people.

"She, uh, that is, her mother thinks …"

Gabe sat up a little straighter. Peter McMillan, a fast-moving workaholic real estate investor with holdings all over the world and, therefore, a multimillionaire, was stuttering! Gabe paid attention. This was one for the books.

The man cleared his throat and started again. "Her mother talks to her about once a week. She said Macy's been strange and evasive lately. No comments about classes or friends. She suspects that something is wrong. When she pressed

21

Macy, she said she had to go and hung up on her. That's not easily done. Believe me, I know."

"And what exactly is it you want me to do?"

"Sort her out," Peter shouted. "And fix it! I'm paying for her to go to school in Paris. Okay, granted it's the Paris American Academy of Fashion Design. But I'm paying a small fortune for her to live in a suite at the Pullman because her mother wanted the best security. So she had damn well better get her butt to class. If she's not going to, then she can come home and go to Boston University, which was good enough for me."

"Let me get this straight. You want me to fly over, see what she's up to, and if she's in trouble, bring her home."

Not gonna happen. There was no way he was making any decisions about the girl's future or trying to make her do that. Hell, he couldn't even get his own son to make some grown-up decisions in his life and he was several years older than Macy!

Gabe offered a compromise. "So why don't I call you once I get there, figure out what's going on, and then you and Macy can figure out the next step. How does that sound?"

He heard a deep inhale and exhale. "Fine! Just go and see her so I can get her deranged mother off my back."

Gabe remembered his first meeting with Peter McMillan, who had summed up the family background in a few emotionless sentences. He was a divorced father of one child, Macy. Her mother was an alcoholic who moved in and out of rehab centers on a regular basis. When she was out, she lived in the family mansion on Cape Cod with Macy. When she was in, Macy stayed with her dad in his condo in downtown Boston.

After Macy announced in her senior year of high school that she wanted to study fashion design in Paris, Peter made the calls and got her admitted to the Paris American Academy. The main benefit of P.A.A. was that all classes are taught in English because Macy spoke no French.

He expected Gabe to make sure she got from Boston to Paris safely and to do it as inconspicuously as possible. Peter was trying to let Macy think she was on her own and exerting her independence, but she was constantly being watched by someone. Security guards at the hotel and school were being paid a little extra to keep an eye on Macy McMillan.

Up until now, it was a great gig.

Once she was dropped off at the departure gate, Gabe would follow her onboard to the first-class section, where he would take a seat in the back row, and then follow her off when they arrived in Paris. He'd make one phone call from the airport to hotel security to have her suite checked out before she got there. He'd watch from the pickup up area until she was safely ensconced in the back seat of yet another limousine. His cab would follow her limo to the hotel and he'd watch her go through the front door where the doorman took her bags and the security guard put her in the elevator.

He'd then check into a five-star hotel and spend the rest of the day and another for good measure, relaxing and eating at his favorite fine restaurants before flying home first class, all on the client's dime. He'd been working for McMillan over a year now and had been to Paris four times. He'd get the call every couple of months and be on the next plane out.

He figured he owed the man one trip where he might actually have to work. "I'll buy the ticket, but all I have is a couple of days."

"The sooner the better!" *Click.*

23

Gabe dashed off an email to his current client, letting her know he had to go out of town for a few days, and didn't wait for the scathing reply he fully expected. He booked his flight online and packed with the efficiency of an ex-FBI agent who was used to traveling at a moment's notice. Then he drove to Philly to catch a red-eye to Paris. Being optimistic, he parked in the short-term parking lot and took the shuttle to the terminal.

He did make one more quick call before he left—to Queenie to tell her he'd be missing the guild meeting. He calmly said he had to leave town to take care of some business and expected to be at next week's meeting. No problem.

He managed a few hours of sleep on the plane, which was so much easier in first class than coach. Sometimes he wondered if he'd ever be able to stand flying coach again. When they landed before noon, Paris time, Gabe was ready to go.

He read the text from McMillan that gave him Macy's schedule, rented a car, and headed for the fashion school, which was located on Rue Saint Jacques. Morning classes were just ending as he pulled up down the block.

Gabe got out and sauntered down the street and back again on the other side, watching for any sign of Macy McMillan. He double-checked the text. She should have been coming out of the building on the right. He waited a few extra minutes until it looked like all the students had departed and then headed to the Hotel Pullman Paris Tour Eiffel, where the 19-year-old was living in a suite with a balcony facing the Eiffel Tower.

He grabbed a coffee and a croissant and then watched the building from down the street. Two uniformed doormen stood at the front and two uniformed security guards were visible inside. He finished his food and deposited his trash in a container in front of a café.

He pulled out his cell and dialed McMillan.

"I went to the school and she wasn't there. I'm standing in front of the hotel. So, given the security at this place, am I going to have trouble getting in?"

"No. The manager is expecting you. He knows you're working for me. He'll give you whatever you need." He paused. "His name's Pierre Dubusson."

"Good. Call you as soon as I know anything."

Gabe walked up to the door and was immediately approached by one of the doormen.

"*Excusez moi,* Monsieur!"

"I'm sorry, my French is very rusty. Do you speak English?"

The man grinned. "Sure do, sir, I'm from Brooklyn."

"Wow. Great accent by the way. You totally had me fooled."

The jauntily dressed doorman shrugged. "Thanks. So what can I help you with, sir?"

"I have an appointment with Monsieur Dubusson. Can you direct me to his office?"

Dubusson, who reminded him of Hercule Poirot, was only too happy to check the computer records for Monsieur Downing. Ms. McMillan had not left her suite this day. They confirmed this with the doorman who added that Ms. McMillan had a guest.

After much head bowing on all sides, Gabe walked toward the elevators, and when the doors started to open, he automatically stepped back. He had almost run into Macy and a guy.

He was a sleazy-looking sort with long black hair hanging in his face and too damned many earrings dotting both ears.

He was easily ten years older than Macy and he had his arm hanging around her neck possessively.

Gabe barely recognized Macy; she looked ghastly. Or perhaps ghostly was the word, considering the amount of dark eye makeup she had plastered on. She was thinner than when he had seen her just two months ago.

He hoped her outfit wasn't indicative of what they were teaching at that fashion design school. Her skirt was about 12 inches long and barely covered her butt. Her halter top looked like she'd taken a long strip of material about 4 inches wide and wrapped it around her waist, crossed it over her chest and tied it at the back of her neck. She had tattoos on both shoulder blades. She was wearing shiny black boots that came halfway up her thigh.

Gabe thought for a moment he was going to lose his lunch. Then he got mad.

Where did these jerks come from? They seemed to breed like rats; rats who made a living off unprotected rich kids who didn't know better yet. It took all his self-control not to simply walk up to this guy and give him his walking papers and maybe a black eye to remember him by. But then what? Macy would probably scratch his eyes out and be more attached to the goon than ever. He'd seen it before. The reality was that you step in to help someone who's being abused and, much of the time, they join with their abuser to beat you off. So he followed them.

They went to the café down the street and ordered coffees and croissants and she paid. They went to an afternoon movie and she paid again. Then to dinner at a restaurant near the hotel and, surprise, she paid for that, too. The only shocker came when she left the sleazy jerk at the door with a shake of her head. He protested but the doorman stepped forward, at which point he shrugged and walked off down the street.

Gabe checked into a hotel nearby and got some sleep. The next day, he watched again to make sure he had the right picture. The loser was back in time for her to buy him lunch at another café, and then she took him up to her suite. He had his confirmation. This guy was no one-off; he was a predator and the reason Macy had checked out of her real life and school.

It was a long three hours waiting for the loser to exit the building. The mental picture of what was happening inside was excruciating. But it was the wrong approach and he knew it. It was also tough to watch the bastard stroll away. Finally, Gabe crossed the street to Macy's building.

With a nod to the clerk, who returned his nod with a smile, he went to the house phone. "Ms. McMillan, may I speak to you?"

"Who is this?"

"My name is Gabe Downing. Your father sent me."

"He doesn't give a damn about me, so why should I talk to you?"

"That's an easy one. You can talk to me now, or you can talk to me while we're on the next plane to Boston, where your father will be meeting you. And he won't be happy."

There was a brief hesitation and then a dramatic sigh. "Come up. It's 1014."

When she opened the door, she looked at him for a second. "Hey, you're the guy who follows me on and off the plane!"

He nodded in silence and swallowed his embarrassment; they had bigger issues.

He walked through the living room straight to the balcony doors. "Wow! This is incredible!" The view of the Eiffel

Tower from the balcony was fantastic. After a moment, he went back to sit on the sofa.

Macy actually looked like a normal kid, just out of the shower. Her face was scrubbed clean, her damp blonde hair pulled up into a ponytail, and she was wearing a t-shirt and boxer shorts. She sat down in one of the chairs and pulled her bare feet up under her.

"You're not going to classes anymore?"

She shrugged, exuding nonchalance.

"Who's the charmer who just left?"

A small look of surprise broke the stone surface of her little face.

"Have you given him any money?"

She flushed and looked down at the carpet and he had his answer.

Gabe sat forward on his seat. "Listen, Macy, the questions are only going to get harder."

She sighed exaggeratedly. "Theo's out of work right now, between plays. He's an actor." Her voice rose defensively. "It's not easy to be an artist, especially in Paris."

Gabe let it pass, knowing she knew how lame it sounded. This girl wasn't dumb but she was a scared kid.

"Are you having sex with him?" Gabe looked her in the eye and asked the question in a quiet, nonjudgmental tone.

"That's none of your freaking business."

"Macy, I want you to understand my position here. I really don't give a shit what you do or who you do it with. But your father asked me to figure out if you're happy here, if you're doing what you really want to be doing."

The pale face fell apart in front of his eyes. She started to cry and then to sob. He handed her his handkerchief and waited. Then she started talking; he listened.

She hated the school and none of the other students would even talk to her. She knew they talked about her behind her back in French. She had come to understand the French for "rich bitch from America."

Her dad didn't care about her or her mom. All he cared about was making money and his business deals. He was the reason her mom drank. She tried to cover for her mom but when Irene passed out and Macy couldn't revive her, she called her dad. He came and threw her into the back of a limousine and told the driver to deliver her to a fancy drunk tank. Sadly, this had happened several times.

Then Peter would take Macy to his condo where she felt like a prisoner. He was never there and she wasn't supposed to leave. A car picked her up every day to take her to school and then delivered her back again.

Macy's face lit up when she talked about her mother. When her mom wasn't drinking, she was wonderful and they had a good time together.

"It's his fault. He doesn't love us. He loves his work and his money." When she had made it through the third waterfall and a box of tissues, in addition to his handkerchief, she whispered, "I want my mom. I want to go home."

He merely nodded. "Good decision."

He asked her for a coffee and while she was in the kitchen getting it, he called her father and, in a low tone, quickly and succinctly told him that Macy was being preyed upon by a so-called actor.

"That's just what Irene was afraid of, that some deadbeat would latch on to her. I guess she's not as crazy as I thought. Bring Macy home."

"And her mother ...?"

"Will meet her at the airport, I'll see to it. Text me the flight details." *Click.*

Gabe would like to have suggested that Peter show up, too, but he didn't want to push his luck.

When Macy returned, Gabe accepted the cup of coffee she offered him. She sat down in the chair with hers and listened while he told her the plan. He told her that they were booked on the first flight out in the morning.

Theo called around six. Gabe answered.

"This is Macy's uncle. Bad news, old man. We're pulling the plug on your meal ticket. She's headed home. Don't ever call this number again or attempt to contact her in any way. If you do, you and I will have a private meeting that I guarantee you will not enjoy."

He put her phone in his pocket. "Sorry about that, but he's going to call back and we won't be answering. As soon as you get home, get a new cellphone and a new number."

Giving Theo enough time to come running, he gently broke the news to Macy that he'd arranged for her to be tested at a medical clinic. Now!

Before his eyes, she turned back into a frightened teenager. He gave her a few minutes to adjust and then added, "And I would expect we'll run into Theo outside. Let me handle it, Macy. Don't say a word."

That was too much; he saw the panic on her face. He took her small hand in his and said, "Listen to me. You're going home. Your mother is expecting you. Hold on to that. I won't let anything happen to you. We will be on a plane for home tomorrow morning. I guarantee it. Okay?"

She forced a smile and nodded.

As he had expected, Theo was pacing back and forth as they exited the building.

"Get in the car." He steered Macy to the car he'd had pulled up to the front of the hotel.

"Macy, *ma cherie*, what are you doing to me?" the young man wailed pathetically. "You cannot abandon me!"

Gabe stepped in front of him and said, "I believe I told you to take a hike."

The much shorter man squared his narrow shoulders. "This is not for you to say, big man. This is none of your business!"

Gabe took one more step toward him. He opened the left side of his jacket enough to let the man see a shoulder holster tucked against his side.

Theo closed his mouth, found his legs, and took off running.

Macy shouted from the car window, "That's right, jerk. Take a hike!"

She laughed. It was a good sound. He got into the car and leaned toward her. "Want another laugh?"

"Sure."

He unclipped his shoulder holster; it was empty. "It's a real pain in the ass to bring a gun into a foreign country." Then he shrugged.

She laughed and clapped her hands. She kept smiling until they arrived at the private clinic where the examinations were not so much fun. Paying what he needed for rapid results, Gabe left there with written proof that she did not have any type of venereal disease and, thank God for small favors, she was not pregnant. She cried quietly in the car as they drove back to the hotel.

So that he could make sure Theo didn't get one last shot at the girl, Gabe slept in her guest room. At six a.m., he marched into her room and threw open the silk draperies that

31

covered the windows. "Let's go, sunshine! We've got a plane to catch!"

As the sunlight fell over her face and she struggled to wake up, he saw what he was looking for—a tiny smidgen of hope in those world-weary blue eyes.

On the way out, they told the doorman she was checking out and would not be returning. Gabe told him that under no circumstances was anyone to go to the suite until the manager had cleared it. He wouldn't have been surprised if good old Theo had gotten his hands on one of Macy's keys. The doorman's eyes widened but he nodded. Gabe tipped him well, looked him squarely in the eyes, and said, "Thanks, Brooklyn."

The man smiled and said in a New York accent, "Ya have a safe flight home, sir."

When they landed in Boston, Macy ran up the ramp looking for her mother. Gabe had never met Irene McMillan. But when he spotted the tall, gorgeous blonde woman, he knew immediately who it was even before she opened her arms to her daughter. He was pleasantly surprised to see Peter McMillan standing back, watching the scene. Gabe was thinking that for all her issues this woman looked pretty damned good. He knew by the way Peter was looking at Irene that he thought so, too. He jerked his head toward baggage claim and Peter nodded.

He met them at the car and handed Macy's bags to the driver; his carryon hanging off one shoulder. Macy's mother turned to him and shook his hand warmly with both of hers. "I don't know how to thank you."

He leaned forward and whispered in her ear as he slipped her Macy's medical reports. "You can thank me by taking better care of her."

She glanced quickly at the folder he'd handed her and when she saw what they were, she gasped. She replied with tears in her eyes, "I plan to do just that. Thank you."

Macy walked up to him before she followed her mom into the back of the limousine, smiling, "So long, Uncle Gabe!"

"You have my number, kiddo."

She threw her arms around his waist and then looked up at him with a hint of uncertainty. He winked at her and nodded. The smile returned and she went back to her mother.

Peter was standing by the car door as the driver helped both ladies into the limo. When they were both inside, he hesitated, and then held out his hand. Gabe took it and shook it firmly.

He knew it was none of his business but he spoke up anyway. "Peter, you have two lovely women there. Don't let them down."

To Gabe's surprise, he nodded and said, "Thank you, Downing." He climbed into the car and it pulled away.

Gabe allowed himself a moment, thinking hopeful thoughts for the family, and then turned back to the terminal. He checked his ticket and realized that he had three hours until his flight to Philadelphia. He hailed a cab and went to his house in Newton. He was relieved that the mail wasn't piled up inside the door; it was apparently being forwarded as he'd requested. He hadn't expected to be in Cutler so long so he took the opportunity to grab a few more clothes and stuff them into his carryon bag. He rechecked the locks on the doors and windows and called another cab to take him back to the airport.

He hadn't listened to his voice mail. Dr. Moriarty could wait a while longer until he got back to town. It was a conversation he wasn't looking forward to having.

Chapter Four

With my takeout dinner in hand, I walked across the back porch from the garage. I never use the front door; it's easier to park and go in the back door to the kitchen.

Our suburban ranch was all the rage when we bought it thirty years ago. They popped up all over the country: three bedrooms, one bath, one car garage, a bare dirt yard, and four stick trees that constituted the entire landscaping "package." Now it has a lush green yard that Harry fought relentlessly to keep free of weeds, and the little sticks are big enough to climb on. And for the record, I don't personally maintain the grass now, but I do write the checks to the lawn service.

Our neighborhood, located at the edge of town, is family oriented and our daughter, Zoey, was always able to walk to school. Parents took turns escorting a little troupe of youngsters the three blocks to school until they were old enough to go unescorted. But even then we never let anyone walk alone. Even in a small town, we never took for granted that bad things can't happen.

The houses closer to the center of town are mostly two stories in the Victorian and Colonial styles. While I do like them, I'm very happy in my rancher and have no plans to move at this point, but who knows what the future might bring?

The Cutler Community Library is located in the downtown area close to the post office. I've worked at the library since I graduated from college. I was able to work part time when Zoey was born but once she started school and a full-time position became available, I took it.

After I was hired, I took a few additional courses in library management at a local college. So, when Mrs. Templeton finally retired after over 50 years as Head Librarian, I was prepared to take over for her but with no intentions of trying to break her record! I was 42 years old when I became head librarian and I have ten years in now. I might make twenty but I can't see beyond that.

I opened the door and set the bag containing my meatloaf dinner on the kitchen counter.

"Harry, I'm home!" I called out as I had for the past 30 years. I got an answer, not from the burly ex-marine with whom I'd shared twenty-plus years of my life, my love, and a daughter, but from a chunky gray-and-white male cat who waited by the door to the basement where his bowls sat. Empty.

"*Yow, yow, meow!?*"

"I know, I know. I'm sorry I'm late. I'll get your dinner."

The resemblances of my cat's behavior to my late husband's were many. Sitting down at the table and waiting for a meal to magically appear before him was one of them, but not one of my favorites.

I poured some dry food into his bowl and filled the other one with fresh water. I placed them on his personalized placemat.

I went down the hall to the master bedroom to change. Harry had added the master bath, now called an "en suite" on the remodeling shows I love to watch, a year after Zoey was born. He realized before I did that one bathroom would not be enough with two females in the house. And he was right. By the time she was three, our Zoey started taking up bathroom time. If we went to check on her, we would hear a little voice from behind the door, saying, "I need some privacy, please."

We were lucky that Harry was based in Virginia so Zoey and I never had to relocate like so many service families do. He did all the traveling back and forth. Harry was a Master Sergeant based at Quantico before he retired. He'd done several tours of duty overseas before being chosen to train and teach at the Marine base in Virginia. He worked for three months and then had a month of leave.

That's when he'd work on one of his home improvement projects. In addition to the master bath, Harry added the front and back porches, remodeled a third bedroom into a sewing room and office for me, and removed the wall between our kitchen and dining room to provide the open concept my remodeling shows had me craving. We had planned on doing more when our time ran out. Now a walk-in closet was no longer on my wish list. I have plenty of closets I can use; I'd rather have Harry back.

I changed into my comfy clothes, which for me means yoga pants and an old Marine Corps t-shirt, stepped into my bedroom slippers, and returned to the kitchen.

When I'd packed up all of Harry's clothing to donate, I couldn't bring myself to part with his worn, soft, and comfy t-shirts. So I gave some to Zoey and continued wearing the rest, as I had when he was here. It was a way of holding on, I suppose, and feeling normal now and then.

I opened the container of food from the diner and chopped up a small piece of my meatloaf.

"There ya go, Harry. A little treat for being such a good boy."

As I dropped the pieces into his bowl, he raised his head briefly and gave me a look that said, "Don't think this makes up for being late. I'm still upset with you," before he accepted the peace offering. The old boy has his pride.

I pulled the TV tray out of the coat closet and sat it in front of my chair, talking to myself, "You should let this sit here, dummy. You use it every night. But what if someone stops over, what if Zoey comes home unannounced, what if Prince Charming rings the doorbell? Oh my, I really am spending too much time alone in this house. No offense, Harry."

After pouring a glass of red wine, I filled my plate with the wonderful meatloaf, mashed potatoes, and green beans from Sylvia's and warmed it in the microwave.

The wine, by the way, is a pinot noir from California. Much to the dismay of our local wine shop owner, Vinnie Grath, who has been trying without much success to expand my palate and my horizons; I continue to buy a white zinfandel and a pinot noir every few weeks, as long as the price is under $10. Despite his efforts, I enjoy just one glass of wine at the end of the day and almost anything will do.

I settled down in my chair with my dinner and wine in front of me and clicked the remote.

"Hurry up, Harry, or you'll miss the start of *Jeopardy*," I shouted to the cat; now washing up after enjoying his meatloaf. "It's harder to guess if you don't see the categories."

He meandered toward the leather recliner that was separated from my wingback chair (which is also a recliner even though it doesn't look like one) by a small table. On the tabletop sits a lamp, a telephone, a tablet, and a pen. I hate a completely dark room and have that lamp on low every evening as we watch our favorite shows or turned up to high if we decide to read.

Harry jumped up and stretched before settling down for his mandatory post-dinner nap; not to be confused with the post-breakfast, post-lunch nap, or midmorning and early-evening naps.

By the way, lest you think it disrespectful of me to name a cat after my late husband, let me explain. My husband was killed in a hunting accident about a year and a half ago. There, I said it without stopping to breathe.

I can't give you the details, because frankly I didn't ask. When anyone tried to tell me, I stopped them. What I do know is that it was the first day of hunting season and Harry'd left the house at about 5 am. It was 8:30 when Herb pounded on the door and then walked in calling my name. All I heard was, "Harry ... shot ... hospital."

I grabbed my purse and he hustled me into his truck. We made record time. He steered me quickly through the emergency room and down another hallway. Even with my heart pounding in my ears, I knew this was the temporary morgue. As if that wasn't enough, Bill Johnson was sitting on a chair in the hallway with his head in his hands, sobbing with tears dripping off his face. Herb stopped short at the double doors.

"Where is he? I want to see him." I must have said it out loud because I heard Herb breathe in sharply. Then he let go of my arm and disappeared. After just a few seconds, he pushed one of the doors open and waved me inside.

Poor Doc Myers was standing next to the gurney, his blue eyes bright with pain. Bless his heart; he had covered the bandages that swathed Harry's head with a knit hunting cap. So what I saw was an orange cap and Harry's rough stubbly face. I could tell he was still wearing his hunting clothes even though Doc had placed a starched white sheet over him up to his neck.

He was laying there as if he were sleeping. That's what we always say, isn't it; that the dead look like they're sleeping even though Harry always slept on his side with his mouth open and snoring softly. I knew immediately where the bullet had gone.

In a matter of seconds I took all of this in and then took a deep breath. I kissed him goodbye and picked up his cold hand. "Damn you, Harry." I whispered.

We had never talked about dying and maybe he had the same vision I did of us growing old together and dying about the same time, peacefully in our bed. It sure wasn't like this, and it wasn't now. We had plans. After I retired from my job at the library, we were going to buy a motor home and travel across the United States. We spent hours going over maps and planning our routes.

Doc handed me a clipboard and I signed some papers without looking at them. Herb stepped up from the shadows and took a plastic bag from Doc's hand. There were some words exchanged about arrangements. I nodded without really understanding what was expected of me.

When we walked back outside the room, Bill was still there. I laid a hand on his shoulder for a moment before Herb led me back outside to his truck. So I knew who and that was enough. I had my own mental pictures of the events and maybe the reality was better and maybe it was worse, but I couldn't bear to hear the words spoken out loud.

To this day, Bill can't look me in the eye and I know he avoids me around town. I don't blame him for that and I don't blame him for Harry. I see his wife from time to time and always ask after him kindly so that he gets the message. I know that in addition to the loss I live with, Bill lives with his own personal albatross of guilt. He killed his best friend since childhood; he needs no recrimination from me. We both know that it was an accident, and we each have to deal with it in our own way.

When I got back home, Diane Murphy came straight out to the truck and collected me. She's been my best friend since grade school, the same to me as Bill was to Harry. She didn't say a word as we went inside although I heard her exchange a few whispers with Herb and he handed her the plastic bag of Harry's personal effects. She made me sit at the kitchen table and handed me a glass of water and a pill. I met her eyes for the first time.

"Swallow it. Take the damn thing, Miranda."

I must have shaken my head because she leaned over me and whispered fiercely. "I have experience with forcing pills down the throats of kids and dogs. You'll take this pill on your own or I'll stuff it down your throat."

I smiled at her sadly and swallowed it. It knocked me out for a few hours. But when I woke up, Harry was still dead.

I would like to say I accepted it with dignity but the truth is that I fell apart. I was in shock for a while and then simply numb.

After the funeral service, as everyone else went to the basement for the chicken dinner the church ladies had prepared, we went to the family plot in the cemetery behind the church. It was just Zoey and me, according to Harry's wishes. As the marble box holding his ashes was lowered into the dirt, I felt like I was watching from afar as someone else buried their husband. That wasn't Harry in that small box, it couldn't be. This wasn't me watching him disappear into the dirt, it couldn't be.

Zoey stood beside me holding my hand. She finally said, "Mom, we have to go inside now, it's starting to rain." I moved beside her and somehow made it through the next two hours as people visited and talked with each other.

I listened as friends shared memories of the good times they'd had with Harry. There were people from his high school class and a few college friends who'd driven hours to be there. I heard them laugh and share stories of the times when Harry did this or that for them.

A Marine Honor Guard from Quantico had marched down the aisle at the church to present the colors as the *Marine Hymn* was softly played over the sound system. They stood at attention at the front of the church throughout the service and stayed on for lunch with us before they returned to base.

Diane and her husband Mark had driven us, and when they brought us back to the house I heard Zoey thank them and tell Diane she'd be in touch.

"If you need anything, anything at all, please just give us a call," Mark had said.

Diane had simply hugged Zoey and then me, holding on tight for a long moment.

I walked into the bedroom and lay down on the bed that Harry and I had shared and fell asleep with my arms wrapped around his pillow. It seemed like ten minutes later when I felt someone shaking me.

"Harry!" I shouted and sat straight up.

Zoey was sitting on the side of my bed. "Mom, it's me. You've been asleep for hours. I wanted to make sure you're okay." Her face was pale, with black circles under her big green eyes, and for the first time in about a week I truly saw how hard this had been on my baby girl.

"Oh, Zoey, I'm so sorry."

I pulled her into my arms and we cried together until there were no tears left. I heard a quote somewhere about how one person is gone from your life and suddenly the world is empty. I finally realized that my girl was hurting as much as I was and I was being selfish by pushing her, and everyone else, away. I promised her I would try to be there for her from then on.

The days passed by and soon the well-wishers faded away. Empty casserole dishes were returned to the names on the little address labels stuck to the bottom, mostly by Diane. She was there from day one. I don't think either of us would have survived without her. Meals appeared, beds were changed, fresh laundry showed up. She popped in and out, not expecting me to talk about it, thank God.

Zoey came out of her room about a week after the funeral and announced that she was going back to school. I was sitting at the kitchen table drinking my coffee and looking through the newspaper, although I wasn't seeing a word on the printed pages.

"I have finals coming up next week, Mom. Then I'll be home for three weeks over Christmas break. Will you be okay?"

I managed a smile. "Don't you worry about me. Your dad would want you to go on with your life. You know how proud he was, we both are, of you." I stood up and gave her a hug.

After a few hard seconds, I stepped back and smiled at her. "Diane thinks I should go back to work. What do you think?"

"I think it would be good for you but only when you're sure that you're ready."

"When did you get to be so wise?" I brushed my hand against her soft cheek. "I'll let them know today."

I took a deep breath. It felt good to be able to make a decision, any decision. Maybe I was finally coming out of the fog.

When I told Diane I'd decided to go back, she was delighted. She had constantly been telling me that they needed me; the place was falling apart. Diane was subtle like a bucket of cold water to the face. She was worried that I would stay hidden in my house because; frankly, I didn't need the job. Between Harry's life insurance and military pension, I had more than enough money, even after paying Zoey's tuition.

I knew I wasn't ready to retire. What would I do with myself all day, every day? Zoey had school and her life in Boston. But it made a difference that I was going to go back to the library because I missed it and because I wanted to, not because I had to. This sudden realization made so much difference in my attitude, not only toward work but to my life in general.

It would take some time to get used to looking out for myself and making decisions based solely on *my* wants and needs. This was different from being the team that had been Harry and me. My whole life had changed in one instant on a cold November morning and I had to accept that it was going to stay changed.

Back to Harry the cat! One evening after Zoey left, I'd gone into the kitchen to scoop out the last serving of Sarah Moore's seven-layer casserole so her dish could be returned to her, when I heard a faint *meow* and some scratching. I opened the back door and a slightly bedraggled cat walked in as if he owned the place, padded straight through to the living room, and jumped up onto Harry's recliner. I followed.

"Uh, you don't live here, cat," I said softly.

The cat, who had clearly intended to nap, opened his eyes and winked at me, like my Harry used to do. *Seriously. No lie.*

My throat tightened but I managed to whisper, "Harry?"

He yawned and put his head down and went to sleep. And that's how Harry came into my life.

Sometimes I wonder what name he was using during his last gig but he always answers to Harry, no problem. I'm not really a cat person, but here's the kicker, my Harry was. They followed him home when he took a walk around the block. He pulled those tabs off of the "free kitten" posters hanging on the bulletin board at the supermarket. But, even when Zoey joined the campaign, I held firm. I had very few rules in the house, but "no pets allowed" was one of the only ones I managed to hold my ground on against the two of them. I knew very well who would end up feeding and cleaning up after the animal they wanted so much.

But it seems that Harry got this one over on me, after all.

And I'm okay with that!

Chapter Five

Before he listened to his voice mails, Gabe allowed himself a few more minutes of peace and quiet. It felt good to be back in Cutler. He felt good about rescuing Macy. He pulled a beer out of the refrigerator and plopped into his easy chair. Then, unable to put it off any longer, he listened to the ten increasingly angry messages from Dr. Moriarty.

The good feelings disappeared.

Why on earth had he let her bulldoze him into taking this case?

After 25 years with the FBI, he'd taken his retirement and run, but not far. Printing up some business cards and running an ad in the Boston newspaper had gotten him established as a private investigator.

The first cases he got were surveillance jobs for jealous spouses who were sure they were being cheated on and wanted evidence. Gabe followed, observed, and then snapped a few photographs that he turned over to the client and accepted a check for his time and expenses.

Then he was hired to shadow Macy incognito to her school in Paris. Apparently he had underestimated her and the kid had made him. He was really off his game.

And now he had spent four weeks trying to track down another freaking college kid. He had gotten his P.I. license to keep from being bored and to earn extra money to add to his FBI pension, but he had underestimated the annoyance factor in dealing with private clients. Even so, he suspected that Patricia Moriarty was in a league of her own.

He should have had a clue from the beginning. He had been sitting in his home office in Newton when the phone rang.

"Downing Investigations. Gabe Downing speaking."

"Mr. Downing. I don't mean to be rude, but let me get straight to the point. I need to see you immediately in my office at The Towers. When can I expect you?"

"Okay, first of all, who the hell is this, and if you don't mean to be rude, then you had better start this conversation over." He clicked off.

When the phone rang the second time, he answered just as he had before. The voice at the other end was the same.

"Mr. Downing, my name is Patricia Moriarty. I'm an author and you may have heard of me. I have a very personal issue that needs handling and … I need your help. There. Was that better?" she snapped.

"Now that we've made the proper introductions, Ms. Moriarty, I have an opening tomorrow afternoon at three."

"It's Dr. Moriarty and clearly you're not understanding me. I need to see you today within the hour. My office number is 312." She hung up.

He had waited an hour and driven into the city, making sure he was at least 45 minutes later than expected. Sure he had heard of Dr. Patricia Moriarty. She was a well-known author of historical fiction. Her books were always number one on all the bestseller lists. Maybe he'd even read a few.

Finding The Towers was easy, too, since it was the most exclusive office address in Boston. He knocked on the office door and was surprised to see that there was no receptionist. A glance at the top of the door showed a tiny security camera. There was a buzzing sound and then a voice.

"Come in, Mr. Downing."

He entered to see the professor, or more accurately, the top of her head behind a desk covered in stacks of papers. Other stacks cluttered every surface in the room. As a person who was close to obsessive in his organization, this room was a nightmare.

"Just move those files and have a seat." Two piles separated and a familiar face, prominently featured on the back of every book she published, peered at him.

With her teased blonde hair piled on top of her head in a hair-sprayed helmet, generous blue eye makeup, bright red lipstick, and large black-framed glasses, it would have been hard to confuse her with anyone else.

"Let's get right to the point, shall we. I need you to find my niece, Amy Moriarty, and the sooner the better for everyone."

"Dr. Moriarty, I don't usually handle missing person cases, but I could refer ..."

"Bullshit!"

"Excuse me!"

"I said bullshit! For the right amount of money, anyone will do anything. I know all about you, Mr. Downing. I know you retired from the FBI and now run a little P.I. firm. I don't want a referral. I want you to find my niece and bring her home."

He sighed and stood up. "I don't believe I can help you. Have a good afternoon."

She stood, too. "I don't understand. Are you saying this is beyond your abilities?" She glared at him.

"No, I'm saying I don't want to work for you."

She was literally speechless.

That was the moment of escape right there. Lord, how he wished he had stuck to his guns and walked out. But she had actually stepped out from behind the desk, changed her tone, and told him the truth about Amy and why she needed to find her.

So he took the job. He figured a week at most. Now he was a month in and Amy was nowhere in sight. He fumed, knowing that if he had access to his FBI resources, he would have had her in a day. Sure, he had a few favors owed to him but he would have been embarrassed to call them in to find Amy Moriarty.

No way was this kid going to get the better of him.

Chapter Six

Walking into the library is still a bit of a thrill for me, even though I do it five days a week, and being a head librarian may not be as exciting or glamorous as you think.

I snagged a cup of coffee from the breakroom and went to my office. After I hung my tote bag on the hook behind the door, I sat down at my desk and opened my computer. A knock on the door was followed immediately by a bright red head.

"Hey, Lucy, what's up for today?"

Our full-time clerk smiled at me, causing her freckles to pop, and waved a fistful of checks. "It's Friday! Happy Bank Day!"

I stifled a sigh. Now don't get me wrong. Very little of our budget comes from overdue books and I certainly appreciate all donations. The people of Cutler appreciate the library and support us. But banking isn't one of my favorite tasks; I'm a librarian, not an accountant.

She ignored my badly disguised lack of enthusiasm and pulled up a chair next to me. I handed her the bank deposit book and started logging in the checks one at a time on the computer while she filled in the deposit slip. She commented on a few of the names and made notes of any we didn't already know. When the deposit was ready and the checks were stamped, I tucked the packet into my tote bag.

"I'll drop this off at the bank at lunchtime."

"Want me to get started on the thank-you notes?"

I knew by the tone of her voice that it was my turn. "It's my turn, isn't it?" I asked cheerily. "I've got it. You have the newsletter and the Marjory Reardon signing on your plate, right?"

She nodded with relief. "Yes, there's a lot going on right now."

"Well, let me know if you need me, Luce. I'll buzz you if I get stuck on a name." I pulled a stack of library note cards from the drawer.

She hesitated and I knew immediately something was on her mind so I looked up at her.

"Have you read the new Amanda Quick?" she almost whispered.

I leaned forward. "No, is it good?"

"OMG!" She clutched her chest with one hand. "It's her best yet. I swear I was up until almost two."

"Wow, okay. That's coming in our next shipment, isn't it?"

She grinned. "That's why I mentioned it. I'd lend you my Kindle but I know you have to hold the actual book in your hands." She leaned forward and lowered her voice. "There are three copies coming. I checked."

I smiled up at her enthusiastic face and wiggled my eyebrows. "Thanks for the heads up. I'll set aside a copy for myself when they get here. There should be some perks to this job, right?"

There's no point in being a head librarian if you can't get first dibs on new books! Much of my time is spent on stretching our budget like a rubber band until it begs for mercy—asking for money, thanking people for money, making sure our money is being used where it's most needed, and so on. Thanks to a dedicated group of donors who answer our cries for help, we are able to fill in most of the gaps left by the annual budget awarded to us by the town council, even though it seems that the first place they look to cut each year is the library.

We try to send out thank-you notes for every donation. Lucy does it most of the time but we agreed it was better for me to send a personal note every now and then. Fundraising lesson one: never take people for granted. She'll also make sure the names make it into our newsletter (lesson two), which is another way we reach out to our patrons for support and let them know about the special events that are coming up.

Our part-timers, Janie and William, love figuring out new ways we can use the library beyond the weekly children's reading hour and the occasional author appearance. It's a wonderful cycle of providing services and reaching out to gain support so we can buy more new books and anything else we need that's not covered by that ever-shrinking budget.

We are especially blessed to have these three employees who care more about the library than their paychecks. We also have a squad of wonderful volunteers who show up several days a week to help shelve books in their proper places and occasionally man the checkout desk.

Head librarian isn't an exciting job by any means, although I admit my heart thumps when a new box of books is delivered and I get to open them. Just like Christmas morning, every time. I was finishing up the last of the thank-you notes when my extension rang.

I answered with my usual, "Miranda Hathaway, how may I help you?"

"Yadda, yadda, yadda!"

"Hey, Diane. What's up?"

Diane teaches English Literature at the high school and is first rate at it, although you'd never guess it from her flip and casual manner. Dee Dee's a big part of the reason my daughter is now working on her Ph.D. at Boston University in English Literature.

"I want to ask you to the prom."

I went along with the joke. "Honestly, you can't get a better date?"

"No, I'm serious. Well, a little bit. Would you like to come over tonight and take some pictures of Ethan in his tux, and his date, for me? Please, please. You know I take terrible pictures. I'll buy your lunch next time. I am not above a little bribery."

This was an easy one compared to some other things she's gotten me into over the years. "And I am willing to be bribed. I'd love to take some pictures for you and Ethan. But where's Mark?"

"He's leaving this morning for his weekend in the woods with his buddies. The dates for this annual trek into the wilderness are etched in stone and *cannot be changed*." Her emphasis on the last three words indicated to me that she was repeating her husband's pronouncement. "They have a campsite reserved up north at Lackawanna State Park. He looks forward to this all year so I can't ask him to stay home."

"Sure then, no problem! What time should I come over? And hey, who's Ethan taking?"

"Gwen Anderson from across the street. Her parents are Becky and Todd. Ethan suffered for weeks before he got up the nerve to ask her. He was driving me nuts!"

"I know Gwen. She's a beautiful girl, but kind of quiet and shy, right?"

"Right, so my equally shy son, who's had a crush on her since elementary school, is taking her to the prom." She cleared her throat. "I am so damned happy for him."

52

The relieved, soft-hearted mom moment only lasted a second and then my girl was back. "And thank God he manned up because I thought I was gonna have to march over there and ask her for him."

I laughed out loud. "I can't think of anything more humiliating than that. Can you even imagine?"

"That's pretty much what Ethan thought." She chuckled, and then added firmly, "It's my job as a mother to provide motivation, one way or another."

That made me laugh again as I pictured Ethan's little Harry Potter face when his mom threatened to walk across the street and invite his date to the prom for him.

"Okay, what time should I be there?"

"Just come over around six. They're going out for the traditional pre-prom dinner with a bunch of other kids so they're leaving early. Prom starts at eight and I have to be there, too. Judy Smythin and I volunteered to chaperone since both our husbands are out of town."

"I'll be there." As I hung up, I shook my head. Did I think Diane would have actually asked Gwen for Ethan? No, of course not. Well, probably not. Good God, I hoped not. But I was really glad it hadn't been put to the test.

I went to the breakroom to refill my coffee and noticed Andy was settled into one of the comfy leather chairs in the corner of the reading room. I left my mug on the counter and quickly snagged a couple of books out of the stacks.

I've noticed he tends to pick out western mysteries. I even admit that I might tend to look for new ones in that category with him in mind when I'm placing an order.

Sometimes I sit down for a minute and talk to him. Yes, it's mostly a one-sided conversation; actually, it's totally a one-sided conversation. Today was no different.

"Hey, Andy, how are you doin' today?" He looked up from his book.

"I just got some more Tony Hillerman books and a couple of those Craig Johnson ones that you like. Ya know, the Walt Longmire mysteries?"

At that his eyes moved to the small stack of books that I'd placed on the coffee table in front of him. He leaned forward to pick up one of the books.

"Well, time for my coffee break. I'm going back to the breakroom. If you'd like some coffee, please help yourself. I think there are some donuts there, too!"

At first I wasn't sure if he understood me, but now I know he does. I stuck my head into the breakroom a little while later and he was seated at the small table nibbling a donut with a hot mug of coffee and a sports magazine in front of him, the small stack of books safely tucked to one side. He was making himself at home and that's exactly how I'd hoped it would work out.

It's not just me, either. I've discovered that our quiet homeless vet can often be seen listening while someone shares their life's struggles. As he sits at the counter at Sylvia's Diner, one of our local elderly will slide onto the stool next to him and share their senior ramblings. Although Andy doesn't speak much, he nods and turns his head to let them know he's listening.

His presence here goes beyond reminding us to help others but quietly absorbs our angst as well. You can tell him anything and know it won't be repeated. Freud would have a field day, as we like to say.

That reminded me that he had spoken to me at guild the other day. What was it he had said? Something about someone not being good? At that moment, one of our volunteers approached me for help and whatever it was flew out of my mind, again.

So, after I got home from work, I changed, fed Harry, and ate a sandwich before I grabbed my Nikon digital and headed out the door.

"See ya later, Harry. I'll be back in time for *Jeopardy*. Don't worry."

"*Neow, neow!*"

"No wisecracks, mister. And you better take a nap because when I get back, I'm gonna kick your butt!"

I walked the three blocks to Harvest Street, remembering Zoey's prom nights that already seemed so long ago.

Diane was on her front porch. She pointed across the street, where Becky and Todd were busy taking pictures of Gwen and Ethan in their yard: in front of the tree, in front of the flower bushes, standing on the front steps. Todd was shooting and Becky was fussing with Gwen's hair, Ethan's tie, etc.

We stood there silently watching the production.

By the time the kids walked across the street, they were already late to meet their friends, so I snapped a couple of shots on the front porch and in front of the flower-covered trellis in the side yard while they complained and fidgeted. And off they went.

"Maybe Becky will give you copies of some of their … hundred or so … shots." I couldn't resist teasing Diane. "You know, to kind of round out the five I came all the way over here to take?"

"Ha ha! Come in for a glass of wine before I get dressed for the prom?" She giggled, "Boy, it's been a while since I've said that."

"Thanks, but I can't stay long. I promised Harry I'd be back in time for *Jeopardy*."

Her face filled with silent concern. "Mandy, you do know that Harry is a cat, right?"

For the record, she's the only person on the face of the earth who calls me by my childhood nickname and I'm the only one who calls her by hers.

"Sure, but we take our *Jeopardy* very seriously."

"Oh, honey, you so need a social life!"

My eyes narrowed. "Not one that consists of chaperoning a prom, thank you very much!" I added quickly, "You go and have a good time. I remember our senior prom and how unhappy you were." Okay, it was a less than subtle change of subject but she went for it like she always did.

Her eyes closed. "Oh my god, Mark and I had a big fight the week before and he took Alice Evans. I was so mad and so jealous I couldn't see straight. I went with Steven Stine because I knew he and Mark were always competing for awards and stuff and hated each other.

"When we were dancing, our eyes met and Mark planted a big wet one on Alice. So, naturally, I kissed Steven long and hard."

"Naturally." I resisted the urge to mouth each word with her, since I knew the scene by heart.

"The day after prom, Mark came over to my house and apologized for everything. He told me that he realized after seeing me with Steven that if he didn't suck it up and apologize for being a jerk, he'd lose the only girl he ever wanted." She sighed with contentment and drained her glass.

"And it worked!"

"Twenty-eight years and counting ..."

I laughed out loud. "I was there at the time, actually, and you do know that I've heard that story a thousand times, right?"

Diane was completely unfazed. "Sure, but I still love to tell it so you have to listen a thousand and one." She shrugged. "And now our kids are going through all this crap."

"I have to remind myself every time Zoey's heart gets broken that it's all part of the process."

"She'll meet the right man one day."

I put down my glass and stood up. "Okay, on that motherly note, I'm going home. And I'm glad I set my DVR to record *Jeopardy*. I'm gonna need a distraction."

Diane leaned in for a hug, "Love ya, girlfriend."

"Me too! Now go have fun at the prom!"

Chapter Seven

Gabe resumed his stakeout routine. It was going to be either Judy Smythin or Taylor Perryman. He didn't know Taylor but he knew that her husband was the local Chief of Police.

So he spent most of his evenings watching the Smythin house because he really didn't think Amy would have the nerve to break into a policeman's home.

Gabe had taken a short-term lease on a small apartment above the wine shop in the downtown section of Cutler. It was convenient in more ways than one. He enjoyed a cold beer every now and then, but there was nothing like a good bottle of wine. In fact, he had a wine cellar in his basement back in Boston with a nice selection of wines he had picked up as he traveled the world.

Gabe had gotten to know his landlord and the owner of the shop fairly well and often stopped in for lively discussions on the pro and cons of imported wines versus domestic labels. Vinnie, whose shop sold mostly American wines to suit the locals' tastes, was enthralled by details of Gabe's collection, which included bottles from famous international wineries.

The apartment was also close to Sylvia's Diner, where Gabe took most of his meals, and only two blocks from the quilt shop. He had joined the Quilt Guild as a way of gleaning information. If anything was happening in this town, those women knew it and discussed it at length while they quilted.

He was almost grateful to his ex-wife. She had goaded him into learning something that she enjoyed, claiming that they never did anything together. His choices were quilting or yoga; he'd chosen quilting after she had the long-arm quilting machine delivered to the house. As he watched her struggle to master it, he decided to read the manual and told her to move out of the chair. A few minutes later he was buzzing along, making beautiful and graceful stitches in the practice material they had stretched over the frame.

He never guessed that this knowledge would help in an investigation. And he also never guessed that a month later she would leave him for her yoga instructor.

When he remarked at the Quilt Guild that he could operate the long-arm quilting machine, Queenie had immediately taken him to the workroom.

When they came out, Queenie happily announced, "He knows what he's doing."

So now Gabe's responsibility at Queenie's was to quilt the projects that had piled up in the workroom. He worked closely with the other quilters and they chose the designs that they wanted. He actually enjoyed being able to complete the projects. Having unfinished things lying around put his nerves on edge. If you start it, finish it!

This was certainly a topic that caused tension between him and his son. Kevin was 26 years old and still didn't have a clue what he wanted to do when he grew up. He got a bachelor's degree in Management and Accounting from Yale, then a master's in Business Administration from Penn State. Kevin was currently working in a coffee shop in Seattle. Gabe could hardly bear to think about it.

Kevin had started a job in Pittsburgh for a prestigious accounting firm, but hated the nine-to-five routine. Great city, great salary, but he hated it. He'd saved a little money, bought a ticket, and off he went. He called regularly to check in but their conversations were awkward and uncomfortable.

Gabe had gone through college in the ROTC program and served four years as a Lieutenant in the Air Force before being accepted for FBI training school. He'd spent 25 years building an impressive record and received numerous citations and awards for his service. He worked hard to earn his pension and the right to enjoy his retirement years. Gabe wanted to continue to be supportive of his only child but it was pretty hard to do that when the boy had no clear direction for his future. It was also hard not to be annoyed, even angry, at the advantages Kevin had been given and tossed aside.

He thought about Kevin a lot as he watched the Smythin house hour after hour. He started to wonder, too, if he should have stayed in Boston and followed up on the other lead.

Gabe wasn't the only one watching the Smythin house and daydreaming.

The girl watched Judy Smythin and her kid (What was his name? Oh that's right, Tommy, after his dad.) from her rental car which was parked about a half a block down the street under some trees. She could see them clearly, but with the sun and the trees, they wouldn't be able to tell for sure if anyone was in the car. Not that they would have even bothered to look. In this burg, people were far too trusting.

She watched while Judy snapped photos of the boy in his tuxedo and the girl in her pretty pink prom dress, first separately and then standing together.

By the way he put his arm around the girl and pulled her close, she was pretty certain this wasn't their first date. Instead of holding her gently at her waist, his hand was clearly on her hip. There was a familiarity in their looks and touches that only someone who'd never known that closeness would notice. She watched as he pinned the flower on the bodice of her gown and his hand gently brushed her breast. He looked into her eyes with a smile at that touch and she closed her eyes for a moment. But Judy didn't notice; she was too busy snapping photos.

The girl pinned the boutonniere on his jacket and kissed his cheek, holding on a little too long. Again, Mom didn't see it. The light breeze carried the woman's gushing voice to her. When the limousine pulled up, she watched the couple jump into the back with some other couples.

Judy waved them off, still snapping pictures, wiped a tear from her cheek, and rushed into the house. A half-hour later, she came out in a blue cocktail dress and heels. She clambered into the silver SUV and took off. Finally!

It was certainly nothing like Amy's senior prom night. She'd told her date she'd meet him there and slipped out of the apartment in her dress, not that Aunt Patricia would have noticed anyway. She'd hailed a cab; no one was around to take a picture. Jeffrey's mom had come to the ballroom at the hotel where the prom was being held and taken a few snapshots. She'd tried to make a fuss over her, but Amy saw the pity in her eyes. The woman had sent her a picture; she still had it somewhere. She took a sip of hot coffee to dispel the memories. There was work to do.

The silence was a relief. She drove to the end of the street, made a right, then another, so she could park in an alley behind a tall line of hedges directly behind the house. She crept through the yard to the back door. The sun was going down but it wasn't quite dark. She had to be careful.

She was willing to bet that there was a spare key under the flower pot or doormat. Ah, they were tricky. It was above the doorframe. She smiled and quietly let herself in. No need to screw around checking for an unlocked door or window here.

Once she had softly closed the door, she scanned the layout. She was in the back of the two-story house; she assumed the bedrooms were upstairs. Moving slowly into a small hallway, she looked to her left and saw a kitchen. To her right was a formal dining room. She continued to the front door and turned back. The living room was now to her right and the left had a closed door. She opened it slowly to see what appeared to be a den and office combination. The staircase to the upstairs was centered on the front door, as it was in most Colonial-style houses built in the 1940s.

She went up the stairs and walked down the hall, opening each door and glancing inside. On the right side, there were two bedrooms with a bathroom in the middle. To the left was the master bedroom and she could see an open door to what appeared to be a master bath.

The room she wanted was the second left; it would have to be the last damned door!

It was getting dark outside and she opened her cellphone to shine the light around the room, keeping it low. She didn't need any nosy neighbors calling the cops.

A countertop was built into one wall, with a sewing machine centered on it. Against another wall were stacks of bins and boxes, obviously holding fabric, batting, and other supplies. A large piece of felt fabric hung on a third wall with a floral strip-pieced quilt in progress hanging on it. The fourth wall was built-in cabinets, floor to ceiling. She went for the cabinets.

Her mind was racing. *Where would I store a family heirloom, and my prized possession, assuming I'm dumb enough to keep it at my house?* She looked up at a long white box on the top shelf. *Bingo.* She pulled it down.

Her breath quickened as she opened it, separated the tissue paper, and saw the green skirt. She was one of only two people in the world who suspected that the skirt held a family secret.

She picked up the skirt with her gloved hands and tried to think like Hannah Haddon. Where would she have hidden something in the skirt? The waistband was really thick and seemed well padded. She pulled a seam ripper from her pocket. Those sewing classes she had taken in high school, and her aunt's fascination with old textiles, had left her with too much respect for such pieces to rip the seams apart. It had to be done but the skirt didn't have to be ruined.

She turned the skirt inside out and sliced along the seam of the waistband, then pulled out the thick batting. When her fingers hit something hard, she pulled. A long strand of perfect pearls came free. She actually put her hand over mouth to keep from screaming with excitement. She took a deep breath to calm down. *Keep working.*

If there was one item in it, there might be more. She used her small sewing scissors to slice through the thickest puffs of batting, pulled them out, and squeezed each piece. She was almost the halfway around the skirt when she felt something through the batting. A blue stone earring gleamed under her cellphone light. She started to work more quickly and sliced until she found the other earring.

Ohmigod, Amy sat down on the floor looking at the treasures: a long strand of perfect pearls and a pair of sapphire earrings. She didn't know whether to laugh or cry. It was simply overwhelming. She had been right!

Gabe decided to check the house, maybe wait inside a bit to see if Amy would show up. Between the senior prom and Judy's husband's camping trip, this was the best chance she was going to get. He'd figured that she'd wait until it was truly dark to make her move.

He slipped around the back of the house and found the door unlocked. His senses immediately went on alert. He stepped into the hallway and stopped to listen. He caught a small noise upstairs. She was here! He moved to the staircase and did his best to creep up the damned creaky stairs.

What was that noise? She put down the skirt. Someone was coming. *Too late, sucker, I'm done here.* She moved to the window and opened it as quietly as she could. She jumped to the tree branch outside.

He heard the window opening. To hell with being quiet, he took the hall in long strides and shoved the door open in time to see the slender black figure disappear. *Damn it!*

He ran to the window and reached, catching the sleeve of her jacket. She leaned away from him, pulling herself toward the center of the tree and he almost fell out the window. He heard a giggle as she slipped out of the jacket and shimmied down the tree like a monkey.

The little vixen gave him a cheeky wave as she disappeared down the alley into the darkness. He was left hanging out of the window with a black windbreaker dangling from his hand. He cursed.

No one had mentioned that she was a freaking gymnast. Gabe's pride was more than just a little wounded; he couldn't believe he'd had her and let her get away.

Being a private investigator and no longer a federal agent meant that he had to act differently than he would have in the past. He sure as hell wasn't gonna shoot her!

Chapter Eight

As usual, we were all busy chatting when Queenie stood and tapped her water glass with a pen, "Your attention, please. The weekly meeting of Cutler Quilting Guild Number One will now come to order."

Queenie waited for our complete attention before she continued.

"Before we start our work today, I'm afraid I have some rather unsettling news to share." She drew out each word to achieve full dramatic effect.

Five sets of eyes were now glued to her face. "You may have noticed that Judy is not here. I'm sorry to report ... that someone ... broke into her house last night."

A general chorus of "Oh no!" and "No way!" combined with gasps of disbelief quickly turned into a hubbub of dismayed babble.

"Quilters, please. Settle down now," Queenie ordered. "Anyone who's ever experienced anything like that knows what a terrible ... violation it is. However, in this instance, it could have been much worse."

At that comment, everyone went silent, waiting her out. "They didn't take anything!" Her voice boomed. "All they did was rummage through her quilting room until ..." she paused and shivers actually ran up my spine, "...they found her lovely trapunto skirt and ..." She paused again.

"For the love of God, Queenie, just tell us!" That was Brittany, who had not yet learned to be patient when Queenie's in performance mode.

The rest of our little group sighed in unison knowing that her outburst of impatience would not speed things up at all. Brittany would learn this the hard way as we had over the years. She's a wonderful person and a truly inspired quilter, but our Queenie must be allowed her moments.

Our leader's slightly wobbly chin rose and, with her lips pressed firmly together, she stared Brittany down. "As I was saying ..." She cleared her throat. "The intruder found her vintage heirloom trapunto skirt and ... tore it apart."

That started us up again but she let us have a few minutes before she *shushed* us.

"I don't know what to make of it, I truly don't. But, on behalf of the guild, I would make a motion that we offer to repair the skirt for Judy if it is at all possible, depending on the extent of the damage, of course. May I have a second, please?"

To everyone's surprise, Gabe was the first to respond. In his very male voice, he called out, "I second." Everyone else nodded in agreement.

"Thank you, Gabe." Queenie's voice softened and she actually fluttered her eyelashes at our only male quilter, with his crisp white hair and serious blue eyes, before she returned to business. "May I have a show of hands, please?"

We all raised our hands and unanimously agreed to help Judy in any way we could.

We're still getting used to Gabe. It's not just that he's kind of cute for an older guy, but it's mostly that none of us have ever worked with a male quilter before. We knew they existed and were creating stunning designs, since each of us subscribed to at least one quilting magazine. Queenie had been introduced to a male quilter at a state conference but it was quite a surprise when one showed up here, asking to join our guild.

It was awkward to say the least. At his first meeting, the women didn't chat as freely as usual and I'm sure he felt that every stitch he took was being watched. After struggling to piece together a simple pillow top that week and the next, he confessed that he would really like to take over the backlog of work that was piled up by the long-arm quilting machine.

Most of us use the smaller sewing machines where we quilt in small sections and then sew the sections together. The Moore sisters didn't even like those, preferring to hand quilt everything. If you visit their charming Victorian on North Street, you'll find no less than three large quilt frames positioned throughout the house holding works in progress. In addition to their own projects, they quilt for friends who prefer hand quilting but don't have either the time or the patience for it. The twin sisters are truly artists with their needles.

The one thing we all agree on is a dread of the "beast" that is the 12-foot long-arm quilting machine that lives in Queenie's workroom. Yes, it can quilt an entire piece in a few hours. But it's also intimidating for everyone except Queenie. With the handlebars that moved the needle, it looked more like driving a motorcycle than creating a family heirloom. I'm just guessing here since I've never even been on a motorcycle!

So we'd gotten into the habit of putting together our larger quilt tops, batting, and backing, and piling them up on the chairs near the monster. When Queenie had time, she'd let us know and we discussed our patterns for the quilted areas. She would then do an amazing and speedy job of finishing them for us. At the risk of sounding, well, mean, we've all been careful never to ask her how *she* really felt about it, since the rest of us were quite happy with this arrangement.

So, while the rest of us were surprised at Gabe's offer, Queenie was no doubt the most hopeful about getting some help with the backlog of unfinished pieces cluttering up her workroom. While she and Gabe disappeared through the pale blue draperies into the workroom to check out the machine, we all crossed our fingers. A sigh of relief went around the room when they came out smiling.

Queenie nodded. "Okay, you scaredy-cats are off the hook for now. He knows what he's doing. You can work with Gabe on your patterns for the long-arm."

I know it's not politically correct these days, but finding out that his interest might be anchored in the traditional male fascination with power tools relaxed our group and he is now cheerfully accepted.

For the next hour, we attempted to work on our individual projects but, needless to say, Queenie's news put a bit of a damper on the group. Eventually, we all gave up and the conversation went back to Judy's break-in. We started to speculate about who would have done such a thing and why?

I held back, as I have been known to do, and waited to see if anyone else would have the same thought I'd had.

"Hey, wait, Judy's skirt was featured on the calendar, wasn't it?" Brittany finally asked.

After a minute of stunned silence, a copy of the calendar was pulled out and quickly consulted. We had put together the calendar to generate some income for our charity projects and to promote Queenie's Quilt Shop. Each month featured a different quilted piece owned or made by our members, along with a brief history of each one. Sometimes the directions for a particular patch or pattern were included.

Sure enough, the lovely green trapunto skirt was featured on the June page with Judy Smythin listed as the owner. A brief history of the skirt explained how it had been left to Judy by her maternal grandmother.

For those who are not familiar, the word "trapunto" comes from the Italian for "to quilt," and is a method of quilting that is also called "stuffed technique." A puffy, decorative feature in a quilt, trapunto utilizes at least two layers of fabric. The underside layer is slit and padded, producing a raised surface.

I found myself exchanging looks with Gabe as the other women continued their discussion. No one had any suggestions to make on why someone would want to destroy a family heirloom.

Finally, Queenie took command. "Well, I think that's about all we're going to accomplish today, folks. So let's wrap it up." We quietly loaded our stuff into our tote bags and filtered out.

As we met by the door, Gabe's eyes met mine. Suddenly, I had the feeling that he knew more about the break-in than the rest of us. But then he smiled and it was gone. I filed it away for future consideration, because that's what we librarians and amateur sleuths do.

I was walking to my car when I heard a voice behind me. "Laura Jenkins." I turned to see Harriet and Sarah hurrying after me. "Pardon me?"

Harriet, the older of the twin sisters by three minutes, took the lead, as usual. "I said, Laura Jenkins. You were wondering who might have a grudge against Judy."

Harriet eagerly moved forward. "She wanted to marry Tom Smythin ever since …" She looked to her sister.

"Second grade."

"Second grade. She decided he was hers and that was that." Harriet shook her head. "When he took up with Judy junior year, she was …"

"… devastated." Sarah finished.

"But, for heaven's sake, that was a long time ago!" I looked at them doubtfully. "She can't seriously still be holding a grudge."

Harriet nodded intently. "Revenge is a dish …"

"… best served cold," Sarah finished.

"That isn't cold, it's frozen."

They stared me down. "Fine." I sighed. "I'll check into it."

"Oh, and don't forget," Harriet added quickly, "last year Laura wanted Queenie to put that raggedy old quilt of hers in the calendar."

"That's right," Sarah confirmed.

"And she was pretty insulted when Queenie offered to restore it for her or show her how."

Now they had my attention. "I'd forgotten all about that. So you're thinking that Judy won again when her skirt made it into the calendar?" I still remained dubious. "But she wasn't the only person who was turned down. There had to have been at least 30 people who brought stuff in for consideration when we were putting the calendar together."

Sarah shrugged. "You know, she never married."

I came into the house through the back door and was greeted with a soft, "*Heow*," as the cat rubbed against my ankles.

I reached down and patted his head. "Hi, Harry."

He turned and sashayed to his dishes, sat down, and waited.

"Okay, sweetheart, give me a minute."

After filling Harry's dishes with water and cat food, with a sprinkle of tuna on top, I went to the bedroom and changed before setting up my tray table in front of my chair.

I scoured the inside of the refrigerator and found a piece of leftover lasagna. While it heated in the microwave, I poured a glass of cabernet that Vinnie had talked me into splurging on, and by splurging I mean paying $14.99. I have to humor him now and then so he doesn't get discouraged. Always doing my part to support local business.

I clicked to the local TV channel and dug into my dinner. Harry had already finished and washed so he settled down in his recliner and put his head down on his paws. After catching up on local and world news, I muted the TV and told him about my day.

"There's something going on, Harry."

He didn't take his eyes off the set but flicked an ear in my direction to let me know he was listening. It really was uncanny how much he echoed my dear Harry's behavior.

"Something very disconcerting has happened." I took a sip of the wine which I have to admit was very good.

"You know that I really enjoy the Quilt Guild. These folks have become like family to me. I know it's been really good for me to socialize and do some charitable work at the same time. I needed that, ya know, after my first Harry died." I paused and took a bite. "The point is, I guess, that we all try to be there for each other."

The ear moved in acknowledgment while Harry continued to rest his head.

"Well, you remember that we did that lovely calendar last year to raise funds for our charity work, right? Six quilts made by our members were featured along with six vintage items, including a trapunto skirt owned by Judy Smythin." I paused for effect and realized I was becoming as dramatic as Queenie, heaven forbid! I continued quickly. "Well, apparently someone broke into Judy's house last night!"

71

His head lifted slightly and turned in my direction, showing intense concentration.

I took a few more bites; it was really pretty good for a leftover.

Harry loves a good mystery, which is one characteristic not shared by my husband, who preferred only direct and straightforward everything.

Once my mouth was empty, I gave him the punch line. "But they didn't actually steal anything. They just tore apart her trapunto skirt!"

This revelation rated a deep-throated *Grrowll* from my furry companion.

"I know! The very skirt that was on the calendar. Isn't that just an awful thing to do? They're not a wealthy family, you know, and that skirt was one of the few items of value that has survived for generations. The women in her family have protected and cherished it since the Revolution. And it was beautiful."

I finished my food. "We voted to help her repair it as best we can, of course. Naturally, everyone's upset and kind of nervous."

Harry sniffed his understanding of that.

"The sisters think it might be an old grudge against her but I find it hard to believe that this was a personal attack against Judy. She's such a lovely woman." I drained my wine glass and turned my complete attention to Harry.

"So what if whoever did this saw the skirt on the calendar?" I let my thoughts follow that path. "What if that's the key? Is whoever did this going to go after other pieces that are featured, and why? They do have value but only intact and how would you get rid of an item that could so easily be identified? It makes no sense to rip it apart and leave it."

Harry looked at me with narrowed eyes.

"It's a bit of a leap to think it's related to our calendar, I grant you that." I took my dishes to the kitchen and returned. "Should I say something to the others who have pieces on the calendar? How will I feel if someone else has a break-in? We need to think about this, Harry, I don't know what to do."

I picked up the remote then turned to my furry friend. "And I have a feeling that Gabe knows more than he's telling."

I was rewarded with a soft "*Yeow*."

I knew it. But that didn't exactly tell me where to go from here. "You surely don't think it was him?"

That got me a disgusted grunt.

"No, me neither. Of course not."

I clicked on a Jeremy Brett *Sherlock Holmes* and lost myself in the work of the brilliant actor and his trusty Watson. When it ended, I turned to Harry to see if he had any insights into our problem. He was snoring softly.

I sighed. "I got nothin' either. Let's sleep on it."

So we went to bed.

Chapter Nine

"Who the heck was that? And what was he doing in the Smythin house?"

Amy's head was spinning. She'd barely managed to get back to her hotel room and double-lock the door before falling onto the bed.

He had almost caught her! What had gone wrong? She had done her homework. She had waited until the house was completely empty and planned to be in and out in less than ten minutes—but she sure hadn't planned on going out the window. Thank heaven for that huge tree in the backyard and her gymnastic lessons as a kid. She was certain he hadn't seen her face. As tired as she was, it came to her quickly.

"Aunt Patricia! She's hired someone to track me down. Of course she did! She'd never bother to look for me herself, would she?" It was the sort of job she'd have dumped on Amy herself if she could. "The joke's on you, Aunt Patricia! Your hired man isn't as smart as your niece! So there!"

What would he do now? The white-haired man knew who she was and that she had been in the Smythin house.

Amy looked at the jewelry she had recovered. It still boggled her mind that anyone would keep such a valuable heirloom in their house with no alarm system and the key above the door.

But that was nothing compared to the respect she had for Hannah Haddon. Rolling the pearls in batting and stringing them around the waistband before stitching it to the skirt was pure genius. Placing the earrings in the thickest padding near the seams on each side panel was clever too, because it distributed the weight evenly.

She deserved to be the one to find whatever was hidden in the Haddon pieces. She fingered the pearls as she gazed at the sparkling sapphire earrings. She was the one who had done all the research, although Aunt Patricia would never give her credit for it. And it had paid off!

It was hard to believe that this research had never been done before.

She spent several weeks on false leads. The listing she had stolen showed three families who might have hidden something that came over in 1759. The Hornbakers and the Wilkes families had proven to be a waste of time. Their pieces were either in museums or locked up tight inside the family mansions or simply gone. It wasn't easy to maintain fabrics for a couple of hundred years. She had taken a quick look at the descendants of each family and then moved on. If nothing came of her quest, she would have lost a few weeks of her life. But, if she found even a single piece that had not been found before, it could be, well, life-changing. It was honestly the most excitement Amy had ever had.

It was such a perfect crime because no one knew that the jewels had even been there! She had stolen nothing they could prove was even missing.

As soon as she saw the calendar, she knew she had struck pay dirt with the Haddons. The research notes referred extensively to the English immigrants bringing valuables to the colonies hidden in trunks of clothing and household goods. One of the examples provided was a copy of a note written by Hannah Haddon regarding the shipping of a trunk of possessions to her husband ahead of her own departure.

While the basic research merely hinted at it, Amy had been intrigued sufficiently to spend a few more hours tracking Hannah and her trunk.

She determined that the secret of Hannah's trunk died with her when her ship floundered off the coast of Massachusetts, even though the trunk was safe on shore already. She had tracked down two quilts and one man's shirt. But there was nothing there. It had to be in the women's clothing; it had to be.

And she felt that there was a good chance the treasures, whatever they were, were still there. There was no indication that the family had utilized any additional wealth after the arrival of that trunk. In truth, they struggled for some time as Henry learned to farm in Massachusetts and then Pennsylvania, apparently without the wherewithal to hire more than one or two farm hands.

Cynthia Stanton, his second wife, would have come into possession of the trunk. Surely, she would have made note of such a find, or some evidence of their sudden spending would have appeared.

Amy took her approach seriously. She kept to her routine of jogging two miles a day to stay in shape for a quick getaway. She wore a simple disguise, in case Aunt Patricia had circulated her picture anywhere through her academic circles.

She flushed to think that Patricia might have also branded her a thief. It wouldn't matter that it was mostly Amy's work. When she'd suggested to Patricia that they take a look at the heirloom pieces to see if any of the treasures were still there, her aunt had waved a dismissive red-nailed hand in Amy's face.

"Don't be ridiculous. Are you really suggesting that these items might have remained hidden in plain sight more or less for over two centuries, waiting for *you* to come along and retrieve them?"

After she'd stopped laughing, Patricia added, "Although that's not a bad plot for a piece of *fiction*, I must say." And she made herself a note while Amy stood there, humiliated. So she really had no one to blame but herself that Amy went off to do it on her own.

Once Amy arrived in Cutler, she had spent a good deal of time at the coffee shop and diner. People in the small town were used to chatting freely and she listened, casually taking notes on her phone. It was almost too easy.

She knew better than to go to the only quilt shop in town, Queenie's. One of these locals might have picked up on her knowledge of quilting and raised the alarm. She wasn't quite bold enough to chat with Judy Smythin face to face.

Her disguise seemed to be working. She wore her long blonde hair under a first-rate dark wig that was made with human hair. She was wearing dark-framed glasses instead of her usual contacts. She had stepped up her usual jeans and t-shirt to silk blouses and slacks to make her look older. She also applied a little foundation makeup and lipstick, something she had never done before.

She chatted up the shopkeepers, gradually getting around to antique textiles. When she expressed her interest, she was shown the calendar. She bought a copy; after all, it was for charity.

The trapunto skirt had seemed her best bet. The calendar identified the owner as Judy Smythin and it only took a few minutes' visit with the hotel clerk to find out that Judy worked at Miller's Drugs on Main Street. It was great fun to walk around the drugstore pretending to look at various items while watching Judy interact with her customers.

She hung around until she heard Judy tell the pharmacist she was going to lunch.

"I'm meeting Taylor at Sylvia's, can I bring you something?"

When the woman declined, she left, saying, "Okay, I'll be back in an hour. Thanks for covering for me."

Amy waited until she was sure Judy was down the street before discreetly following. She thought to herself, *God, this place is so boring! Everyone does the same things all the time!* The locals all seemed to gravitate toward Sylvia's Diner, Tex's Tacos, or Main Street Pizza and Sub Shop, day after day.

She waited until Judy was inside and then entered the diner. She walked past the booth where Judy had just taken a seat across from another woman. Her hair was a lighter brown than Judy's but she had the same dark blue eyes, although hers had smudged purple circles under them. Amy slipped into the booth behind them.

They exchanged greetings and the waitress came to the table and took their orders. She returned quickly with two BLT sandwiches and two iced teas. Judy thanked her.

Amy ordered a cup of coffee and a donut, which the efficient waitress delivered in what seemed like seconds.

She overheard Judy say, "I'm so sorry, Taylor, I know Ricky isn't getting any better."

"The doctors have said there's nothing more they can do. They're just keeping him comfortable until …" The other woman picked up her napkin and dabbed at her eyes.

"When are you going out again?"

"I'm going next weekend. Jake has to work so I'll be going alone."

"Darn. I'm chaperoning the prom with Diane Murphy on Saturday night. Tom and Mark are going on their annual camping trip."

Taylor's pale face lit up. "Prom night! Wow, I can't believe Tommy is a senior. I still can't wrap my head around Jessie being in college, either. Where on earth have the years gone?"

"Time does seem to fly. Do you remember Tommy's girlfriend, Julie Sorensen? They've been dating for two years now and they work together at the pizza shop. Tommy does most of the deliveries."

"Sure, I know Julie. When Jake works nights, I sometimes pick up a pizza and take it down to the station. She's a sweet little thing!"

"She is and she works part time and helps with her little sister when her mom has to work the evening shift down at the factory." She sighed. "Now if Jessie would find someone as nice, I'd be a happy mom. She dates a lot but no one serious as yet. Since she's thinking of going for a master's after she finishes her undergrad degree, maybe it's just as well."

"You know what they say, 'You can't hurry love.'" Taylor smiled.

"Jessie comes home most weekends because she's only about two hours away but she said since we're all busy, she'd stay at school this weekend. She has an important paper due next Monday. Anyway, enough about me and mine. I'm so sorry I can't go with you. Let me know the next time and I'll really try to come with you, okay?"

"Thanks, honey, I appreciate it. You have fun at the prom! Boy, does that bring back memories!"

They finished their lunch, paid, and walked outside. Amy watched until they hugged and went their separate ways.

She'd entered Judy Smythin, Cutler, Pennsylvania, into Google and, *voila*, had her home address and phone number in a matter of seconds. And that's how easy it had been!

But now the local yokels were all bent out of shape. Apparently nothing ever happened in this town. Amy went to the diner for lunch, and every conversation seemed to be about the break-in at the Smythin house. She finished her sandwich and iced tea and was about to go to the cash register to pay when a white-haired guy walked in.

Her stomach sank as she realized who it was. That shock of white hair! She tried to put a face to the guy who had grabbed her as she jumped into the tree outside the Smythin place. All she could remember was the glow of his hair in the moonlight. Amy was afraid he'd see the recognition in her face, so she stayed put and quickly signaled the waitress for more iced tea. There was the smallest chance that something about her would jog his memory.

Then there was that guy in camo sitting down at the end of the counter. He really gave Amy the creeps. All he did was walk around town, talking to himself. She suspected he was one of those chronically homeless, mentally ill types. Once she thought she'd heard him say, "Up to no good," as he walked past her.

The white-haired guy was chatting up the heavyset woman behind the counter.

"Hey, Sylvia, how's it goin'?"

"Good, Gabe. What can I get for ya today?"

"What's the lunch special?"

"I made up a batch of my secret chili recipe this morning. Special is a bowl of that plus a burger for $4.95."

"Sounds great! I'll take that and how about the same for Andy down there?" He laid a $20 on the counter.

"Got it! And thanks, Gabe."

The woman came back in a few minutes and deftly placed the orders in front of them. As she set the bowl and plate in front of the homeless guy, Amy heard her say, "Here ya go, Andy." So now all the players had names.

She waited, pretending to be engrossed in her phone, until Gabe left the diner. Then she took a breath, moved quickly to the register, and paid her own bill.

Amy decided right then that she needed to get out of town for a week or two until things cooled down. The more she thought about it, the better she felt. She had somewhere else to go, anyway.

She went back to the motel and packed her bag. As she drove out to the Interstate, she chuckled to herself and mouthed in her best Schwarzenegger imitation, "I'll be baacck!"

Chapter Ten

I was sitting at my desk in the library looking through a catalog of new books and resignedly narrowing down my choices in consideration of our limited space and funding, when there was a knock on the office door.

"Come on in," I said, thankful for the interruption and not caring who it was as long as it distracted me from all the bestsellers we couldn't afford.

Judy Smythin opened the door just enough to slide in. I waved her to the chair in front of my desk and she sat down with a small, forced smile. I saw bags under her pretty blue eyes. Even though she worked full time and had two kids and therefore had every right to be tired, I suspected it was the recent break-in that had taken a toll.

"Hi, Miranda."

I nodded. "I'm sorry to hear about your …"

She interceded for me, waving a hand. "I know. You scarcely know what to call it, do you?" She reached into her carryall. "But that's why I came. I wanted to show you something." She pulled out several pieces of green quilted fabric and laid them on the edge of my desk. Then she turned them over.

I gasped. I couldn't help it. Having seen the skirt at its best, and now seeing the desecration of what had been a family treasure—sections of fabric sliced open and threads hanging loose—brought tears to my eyes.

"Oh, Judy!" I managed.

She pulled a water bottle from her bag and took a swallow, cleared her throat, and lowered her shoulders.

"It does take some getting used to. But like Tom keeps telling me, it's just a thing, not a person."

After a brief moment, she continued. "I brought this to you because the police aren't really interested and I know you're a bit of a detective at heart. And I'd like you to take a good look at these pieces."

I opened my mouth to protest but then simply shrugged. It is true that I have watched all the Sherlock Holmes movies and TV shows at least twice. I did help Susie Jensen find her lost dog a couple of times. I guess that qualifies me more than most in this town. Of course, it's a small town.

"Bring them over to the window." I have a long table there for sorting and unpacking books. We smoothed out the pieces and I bent over to examine them closely.

"Ohmigod!" I looked up at her, my mouth gaping, and pointed. "Whoever did this used a seam ripper on the waistband!" Then I looked closely at the trapunto stitching. "And this trapunto was cut with a pair of scissors!"

She nodded with relief. "Thank you! I thought I was *really* losing my mind." We stared at each other for a moment. "What do you think that means?"

"Well," I narrowed my eyes like Harry does for intense-thinking purposes, "if someone gets cut in a certain way on one of my TV mysteries, they say that the perpetrator had medical training, right?" I said slowly.

Judy responded quietly with what was clearly her own foregone conclusion. "So whoever cut up my skirt was a quilter, or at least someone who has sewing experience."

I swallowed hard. "I just can't imagine …"

"Exactly." She counted off on her fingers. "First, I don't know anyone who hates me enough to cut up my heirloom skirt just to be mean. Second, whoever did this clearly didn't mean to do the kind of damage that would keep the skirt from being repaired. It will never be the same, obviously, but it can be restored. And, third," she paused for effect, and then, despite the seriousness of the discussion, giggled. "Ohmigod, I'm doing Queenie!" She took a breath.

"So it comes down to this—if it wasn't personal and they didn't want to destroy the skirt, then why do this at all?" We both automatically looked down at the pieces of damaged fabric.

She looked so sad that I felt sorry for her but I was also angry that my friend had been violated in this way. Why indeed? I thought of another "why" to add to her list. Why hadn't they just grabbed the skirt and run away with it? We were both lost in our own thoughts for a few seconds.

I saw tears forming in her eyes. "Come sit down with me, Judy. Can I get you some coffee or something?"

"No, I'm fine. I can't stay long. I took a break from work to stop in. I've got to get back to the drugstore."

Miller's Drugs, where she worked full time, was only two blocks away. But she had been distressed enough to leave work to bring these pieces of her skirt to me. Knowing that, it only seemed fair to share our discussion from the Quilt Guild meeting yesterday.

"Do you think this might have had anything to do with your skirt being featured in the Guild calendar?"

Her eyes widened. "I hadn't thought about that."

I nodded. "We talked about it at the group yesterday. Brittany pointed out that your skirt was in the calendar. And, of course, your name was there, too. It would have been easy to get your address. There aren't that many Smythins around here."

We were both quiet for a minute.

I cleared my throat. "Do you, uh, remember Laura Jenkins?"

Her eyes widened. "Sure. We went all through school together. Wait, she had an awful crush on Tom, didn't she? Oh my, you don't think …"

"People do hold grudges, but it's been quite a while." I had another thought. "Say, didn't Tom just get a promotion?"

She smiled proudly. "Yep. Assistant Vice President of Lincoln National Bank."

"Congratulations! Did he, uh, I mean, was anyone, uh, annoyed by his promotion?"

Judy's eyes widened. "Oh, Miranda, I hate having to think this way!" She paused a moment. "Sam Marconi has been there longer. He didn't have any college and Tom has a business degree, ya know? But he and Janet are good friends of ours. There's no way!"

"Of course not." I smiled at her while I mentally added Sam and his wife to my list of suspects. "I'll tell you what. I'll do a little snooping around just to check out some things and that will be that."

"Do you think I should be scared? It may have been dumb luck that we were all away the other night. You don't think the person will come back, do you?"

I put on my reassuring face. "No. That's just the point. Any reason someone had for doing this, it's done." I added thoughtfully, "But, honestly, you might want to think about putting the skirt somewhere safer once it's repaired. It's such a rare piece."

She flushed pink. "I know. I should never have let it lay around my house like that. I'm gonna speak to Taylor about maybe donating our pieces to a museum or something where they can be taken care of properly and other people can enjoy them."

Taylor! I swallowed. "Taylor has that vintage bed jacket, doesn't she?"

I went to my desk and pulled out the guild calendar. Taylor's lovely blue bed jacket was on the March page.

Judy bent over my shoulder. "See? It can't be a calendar thing, right? Taylor's jacket was March, several pages ahead of my skirt, and no one's broken into her house."

Breaking into the house of the local police chief would not be anybody's first choice but I decided not to share that thought right now.

Thankfully, Judy was distracted by her own thoughts as she put the pieces back into her bag. "We're related through our maternal grandmother. The few heirlooms we have were handed down through the generations and split up amongst the Haddon descendants."

She shook her head as if to clear it and grinned ruefully. "I've often wished they'd left us money instead."

I smiled my best plastic smile. "I bet you do." I stood as she headed to the door. "Make sure you drop your skirt off at Queenie's. You know she'll fix it right up."

"I know. She already called me." She hesitated. "Thanks, Miranda."

"I really didn't do anything." I patted her shoulder. "I truly don't think you or your family are in danger but we'll figure this out."

She brightened, "That makes me feel better."

Then she was gone. I was glad she felt better because I certainly didn't.

Chapter Eleven

After lunch, I started checking in a new shipment of books that had just arrived. Seeing the shiny new covers always brought a grin to my face—and the smell! There was something about the crisp clean scent of printer's ink. I could imagine our library members grabbing them up, especially those who couldn't afford to buy a copy at what seemed like ever-rising prices for hardbacks. And I happily stuck one of the new Amanda Quick copies into my drawer to check out later myself.

But even as I catalogued and stickered, the questions ran on a loop in my head, like a song you can't stop hearing. Why did someone break into Judy's house just to rip up her skirt? What did the calendar have to do with it? Or did this have something to do with the Haddon family? And the one that bothered me most of all: Was Taylor's house about to be broken into? Should I say something? Or would that be worrying her with precious little to base it on, and make me look like an idiot if nothing came of it?

All I managed to do was give myself a boomer of a headache and take twice as long as I should have checking in the new books.

About three, break time, I sat down and drank a strong cup of coffee, which usually helps subdue my headaches, infrequent though they are. I closed my eyes and tried to settle my tired brain. Visualization also works sometimes so I tried it: calm blue ocean; calm blue ocean; calm blue ocean ... slow gentle waves; slow gentle waves; slow gentle waves ...

I was almost there, on the beach with the waves hushing me, and the sun warming me, when someone knocked.

"Come in." My eyes popped open and I tried to look alert.

"Hey, Miranda!" Jake Perryman stood awkwardly in the doorway. He wanted to come in but he didn't. I get that a lot, actually, more than you'd expect. I have never figured out why people equate going into a librarian's office with going to the principal's office. I've always encouraged people to stop in with suggestions for books or to discuss their favorite books or authors. I've never been told I'm scary looking.

"I hope I'm not interrupting anything."

"Just taking a coffee break. Can I get you something?" I asked with an encouraging smile.

He shook his head and I waved him to the chair in front of my desk.

"Take a load off, Jake."

"Thanks." He sat gratefully.

The man carried too much weight and it showed in his flushed face, but it wasn't up to me to tell him. In his defense, my office is on the second floor of the library and there is quite a long set of stairs to climb to reach it. Actually, there are 18 steps and I know that because I climb them several times a day and, for some reason, feel compelled to count them every time.

I've known Jake and Taylor since high school, although they were both two years behind me. So many of our friends have moved away; those of us who stayed have become a tightly knit group. Our high school reunions are so small that they usually combine classes from several years at one event.

Jake was a terrific high school football player and played in college as well; but now, about 30 years later, he'd gained weight, but haven't we all?

"So what's up?" I opened, after giving him a minute to catch his breath.

He cleared his throat. "It's about this, uh, thing of Judy's? She stopped by the station and reported the break-in yesterday morning but, well, nothing was taken, and ..."

I nodded sympathetically. "It's not like the police force has nothing better to do ..."

"Thank you!" he said emphatically as he leaned forward with his hat in his hands. "You see, we're trying to break up some gang activity over by the high school. There aren't that many of us and we're stretched thin as it is."

"And nothing was taken; therefore, I don't see what you can do."

"That's the truth of it. But because Judy is Taylor's cousin, she figures I should be, ya know, calling Interpol or something."

"Ah, I see." I flushed slightly, remembering my concerns about Taylor and her own antique textile piece. Was this my chance to say something? Yet I couldn't get the words out. Jake seemed to have a full plate right now.

"I feel stupid asking this but ... you didn't find any fingerprints, did you?"

"We tried."

We said in unison, "They wore gloves."

"At any rate, Judy stopped by my office today to tell me she'd shown you the skirt and you said you'd help in any way you could."

Before I could protest, he raised a beefy hand to stop me. "It's fine, really. Anything you can do to make her feel better. We all understand that a break-in really scares people. What I wanted to ask you is, if you come up with anything, especially if it's remotely dangerous, to let me know first thing. I don't want anyone getting hurt over an old skirt."

"Of course!"

"Thanks." He stood and wiped his brow with a big red handkerchief, and then tucked it back into his pocket. "I'm sure hoping we don't have a professional thief in town, but since they really didn't take anything I can hardly even call it a theft."

I struggled to stifle my grin. His face clearly said the opposite; it would certainly be the most exciting thing that had happened while he'd been on the force.

"Ya know we had that bank robbery." He shook his head, every inch the serious officer of the law. "And now we've got gangs."

I contented myself with a shrug and a serious expression as he departed. I waited until I was pretty sure he was gone before I gave in to a fit of the giggles.

"The Bank Robbery," as it shall forever be known, happened about three years ago. Old Rafe Russell couldn't find the key to his safe deposit box, and the assistant manager at the bank wouldn't open it for him. Despite his explanation that he couldn't, Old Rafe took off in a huff—and returned with a shotgun to blow open the box. He walked in, told everyone to get out of his way, and shot a huge hole in the safe deposit box. If I've heard that story once, I've heard it a bazillion times.

Poor Jake! We're a pretty boring bunch. And low rent, frankly. The only other robbery that I can remember was when a bunch of high school kids, drove down a country lane and took every mailbox for about two miles. Then they threw them all into the local dump. Truth is that no one in Cutler has enough money to own anything of significant value; nobody that I know anyway.

And I'd heard about the "gangs" he mentioned. Seems some teenagers had assembled a makeshift skateboard park out at the high school parking lot. They built ramps and steps that they hauled in their pickup trucks. When they thought no one was around, they set up a course where they would ride until they heard the police sirens. Then they'd load up the stuff and get out of there.

Our locals seem to love their sirens. It would be much smarter to drive over quietly and have a talk with the kids about private property and insurance liabilities, etc. But, in such a small town, even a couple of kids on skateboards could get the police excited.

The town basically exists because of a single employer, the candy factory, which is a subsidiary of a much larger and more famous one. Most of the employees working there do no more than barely earn an honest living.

The point is that being a policeman around here, even the chief, is mostly about parking tickets and the occasional loud party.

It had been hard to keep my mouth shut. All those questions were right there on the tip of my tongue, trying to slip out. A part of me wanted desperately to warn him. But I had nothing to base that on. You just can't throw people's lives into an uproar on guesses and hunches. That wasn't fair either. Maybe Judy would talk Taylor into getting that jacket out of her house, and soon.

It seemed like it had been a long day by the time I slid my key into the lock, opened the door, and called out to Harry.

I almost tripped over him. His ears were laid back and his eyes were squinty. "What is the matter with you?" I asked sternly. "You just put those ears up, mister."

He pranced away from me, all huffy. How did he even know? "I told Judy I would think about it, that's all. I might do some computer research. I'm not sticking my nose into anything dangerous," I called after him.

He didn't mind me talking about a mystery or watching one on TV, but doing something about it was a different matter entirely. Risking anything happening to his meal ticket was unthinkable. So he resorted to silence—his strongest weapon—just like my other Harry.

"Fine! I don't need your help anyway!" I called to his waving tail.

He accepted his dinner in silence and would not touch a bite until I left the room. Men!

Chapter Twelve

When he had gotten over his snit and joined me, we settled in to watch the news. A strong knock on the front door startled us both. I jumped and Harry raised his head. I wasn't expecting anyone and only Diane would have shown up without calling. And she wouldn't have knocked on the front door; she would have walked in through the kitchen and yelled, "Anybody home?"

I looked down at my Marine Corps t-shirt and yoga pants and sighed. God, I hoped it was a salesman so I could just open the door a crack and send him (or her) down the road.

"Hello?" I ventured through the door.

I'm not great with the peephole. Harry always told me to stand back to one side so I wouldn't get shot through the door. I humored him; I've no idea why. No one had ever even splintered the wood.

I heard a deep voice clear a throat. "It's Gabe. If this is a bad time …"

I opened the door. "Not at all. What can I do for you?"

He stood there looking awkward to say the least; he looked at me and then down at the "Welcome" mat. I took the hint.

"Come on in, Gabe. Sorry, I didn't mean to keep you standing there." I stood aside and he stepped in. "Forgive my manners. I don't get a lot of company … weeknights … or anytime for that matter."

He smiled down at me. "I should have called."

Well, yeah! That's not what I said, of course. "Don't be silly. It's a small town, we're not that formal." I led the way to the living room. "Take a seat." I added, "Harry!"

The cat opened one eye, spied Gabe, then took his time stretching before he vacated the leather recliner and moved toward the loveseat against the far wall. I grabbed his blanket off the chair, dusted the seat with it, and gestured for Gabe to sit down. I placed the blanket at the end of the love seat and Harry immediately jumped up. He circled a few times and then lay down and, after a giving Gabe another once over, closed his eyes.

His smile widened. "Well, I hate to put, uh, Harry out."

I lowered my voice. "That's okay. We were about to play *Jeopardy* and he's not so great at it anyway."

Gabe looked at Harry, who now pretended to be sleeping. "Really?"

I kept a straight face and said, "He keeps forgetting to answer in the form of a question."

Then I couldn't help myself. I laughed and he joined me. Frankly, I was relieved that Harry had so graciously vacated his chair. I was afraid he'd make a fuss. I made a mental note to throw him an extra treat at breakfast.

"So you play *Jeopardy*, do you?" He sat down and his eyes went to the muted TV where Alex Trebek was interviewing the contestants.

I felt the flush creep up my face. Damn pale skin anyway. "My husband and I always played when he was home, so I guess it's a habit. And I always learn something new."

He sighed and I noticed, "My wife and I used to play. I understand."

Awkward. "Can I get you a beer or a glass of wine?"

"Wine is good." He followed me into the kitchen.

As I pulled the bottle out of the refrigerator, I asked if he'd met Vinnie.

"As a matter of fact, I'm living in an apartment over the wine shop so I probably spend more time there than I should."

"Vinnie's a nice guy. He talked me into shelling out $15 for this bottle of pinot noir, but it's pretty good." He didn't reply so I prattled on. "Are you hungry? Would you like some cheese and crackers or something?"

He raised a hand. "I'm fine, really."

He waited silently while I filled two glasses and then he followed me back to the living room.

The first round was well underway. Did I mention that I hate not seeing the categories? We each took a sip and sat the glasses on the stand between the two chairs.

"How do you like our little town so far?" I know, lame! I really must brush up on my small talk repertoire. Why the heck didn't he just tell me why he was here? If I hadn't been recording the show, I'd have been quite put out.

"It's a big change from Boston, that's for sure; but I like how people here look out for each other." He hesitated. "Take this thing with Judy. Everyone in the Quilt Guild genuinely cares about what's happening with her. First, it was the baseball mom, and now, the skirt thing." I felt his eyes on me.

I thought for a moment before I replied. "It's the same in town as it is in the Quilt Guild. There's a core of us old-timers who stayed here after high school, but it's shrinking I'm sad to say. So we're trying to embrace people like Vinnie and the other new business owners." I didn't even try to keep the melancholy out of my voice. "Nothing ever stays the same."

"That's a hard lesson to learn and it doesn't matter where you live," he added gently. "I didn't want to intrude at the guild meeting, being new and all; but do you think Judy's okay? Is she scared? Afraid this person will come back?"

He sounded so sincerely concerned that I answered quickly. "I tried to assure Judy that whoever did this had done what they wanted and would most likely not return. I really don't think she or her family is in any danger. Do you think they're in danger?"

"No, I don't. I completely agree with you." He frowned. "I apologize for eavesdropping but I heard the twins mention someone who might be a suspect as we were coming out of guild earlier? Harriet and Sarah seemed rather convinced that this woman might be a person of interest."

"Oh, that was Laura Jenkins." I shrugged. "I've already eliminated her as a suspect."

Stacy Sheriff had come into the library before closing and it dawned on me that the tall, graceful Jamaican woman with warm brown eyes, who cleaned the library twice a week, also did housekeeping for several families around town.

"Hey, Stacy."

She turned to me and flashed her bright smile. In her almost perfect English with just a bit of an accent, she said, "Hello to you, Miz Miranda. I am a bit early today. I am hoping this okay?"

I had to smile back; you just couldn't help it. I know she's worked hard at learning English has even stopped by a few times just to practice. "I truly don't know how you do it. Are you still working for different families around town?"

"Yes I am. I do the cleanin' for Miz Mabel, Miz Betta, and Miz Laura."

"Umm, I haven't seen Laura for a while."

She nodded sagely. "And you won't be seein' her any time soon, I can tell you that. The poor woman got the bad luck. She step off the sidewalk and done up her ankle so bad!" She shook her head and her beaded braids danced about. "She go to the hospital and they wrappin' it all up. She not be wantin' the whole town to know, you see."

"Well, I'm sorry to hear that. When did this happen?" I asked casually.

"I am thinkin' it might be last Thursday, when she go to the market." She frowned briefly but then her face brightened again; it was hard for Stacy to stop smiling for long. "Ah well, now I can do the cleanin' easy enough. She must stay put and out from under me feet." She laughed and I joined her.

I patted her arm. "You're a good person, Stacy."

She shrugged off the praise. "We all do what we can in this world, Miz Miranda."

I nodded. "You take care."

"The Lord, he watch over the likes of me. And you, too."

I suddenly remembered Gabe, who was watching me in silence. I recognized the strategy but didn't mind sharing. "Here's the thing. Laura has a sprained ankle. She's been hobbling around since last Thursday. It wouldn't have made much sense for her to pick this particular time to take her revenge on Judy." It was my turn to frown.

"And she was your only suspect?" he shook his head sympathetically.

"Well, there was a man who works with Tom at the bank. Tom was promoted recently and the other guy has been there longer, and I suspected that he and/or his wife might have been upset about that, but Judy found out that they were out of town all weekend celebrating their anniversary in the

Poconos so that's another dead end. So much for my investigative skills, I lost three suspects in one day."

His eyes crinkled at the corners. "That's pretty impressive work."

"It would be more impressive if I had eliminated all but one of the suspects. And it would have been really great if that one suspect had no alibi." I glanced at the TV.

His eyes flicked to the screen, where double jeopardy was about to start.

I looked at him carefully. "Would you, uh, like to play?"

His face actually lit up, "Really? Are you sure I wouldn't be interfering?"

"No, no problem. I always record it just in case I get a call during the show. I should warn you that this is pretty much what passes for evening entertainment in Cutler."

He flashed me a challenge with his bright blue-eyed gaze. "Okay then, you're on. How do you score?"

"Simple. One point for each right answer. You can bet any or all of your points on final. High score wins. Answers must be in the form of a question." I grabbed the pad from my side table drawer and two pens, ripped off a paper for me, and handed him the pad. I would use the table as I always did. "For final jeopardy, write your answer down."

I grabbed the TV remote to rewind the program back to the beginning.

Okay, it was fun. It always depends on the categories, of course. That wretched Geography gets me every time; I'm actually not half bad at Sports, by virtue of watching TV with Harry (the husband, not the cat) every weekend.

It was a tie going into final jeopardy. The category was English Literature. I smiled. He looked tense. I bet all but one of my points. *Jeopardy* is no place for the timid.

I resisted the urge to pump my fist in the air in victory but it was more satisfying to beat Gabe than it was to beat Harry (the cat), I admit.

"As soon as I saw that final category, I knew I was in deep trouble." He laughed as he picked up his glass, took the last sip of wine and then stood. "Well, I should probably go."

I got up and followed him to the door.

"Thanks, Miranda. That was fun."

I shook my head and laughed. "Clearly, you need to get out more." As soon as I said it, I wanted to take the words back.

A smile played at the corners of his mouth. He lowered his head and kissed my cheek. Then he was gone and my cheek was warm from his lips. It has been a while, but I chose not to go there. And I still had no idea why he came over in the first place.

But I did learn a few things about Gabe Downing that I didn't know before tonight. I know that he's almost as fast a reader as I am because I tend to speed-read the questions. He's very good at Geography and ran the World Capitals category, indicating that he had probably traveled a lot more than I have. He was knowledgeable about wine and answered almost all of the questions under Growing Grapes to my embarrassment (hey, I served the man a $15 bottle of wine!), and knew a lot about Italian Operas. When it came to Government Agencies, I had the sense that he stopped himself and deliberately said the wrong thing a couple of times so he wouldn't run the category. What's up with that?

Anyway, as you can see, you can learn so much about a person by playing *Jeopardy* with them.

Chapter Thirteen

Friday morning as I finished up the bank deposit the phone rang. I answered as usual and all I heard was, "Well." A very unhappy female was on the other end.

"Hi, Diane. How are you?" I knew exactly what the problem was so her tone didn't faze me in the least.

"How am I? How am I?" she responded heatedly. "I cannot believe you didn't call me about this Judy thing. If I'd known this little quilt club of yours was going to be so exciting, I'd have learned how. Seriously!"

"Sorry." But before I could stop myself, I laughed out loud.

"That's it! You think you're so funny. You're buying me lunch, today!"

"Sure thing, Dee Dee, love to."

"Usual?" she demanded.

"Noonish," I answered calmly, just to irritate her.

"Humph."

Precisely at 12:10, I walked into the Town Tavern, our favorite lunch place. Diane was already in our usual booth with two pink cocktails in front of her. I smiled. She frowned, trying to maintain her fit of pique. I gave it about thirty seconds.

"I'm sorry I didn't tell you. It might be a lot of nothing," I said as I slid in across from her. "It makes me realize though how desperate we are for excitement around here. And you have to remember nothing was actually stolen, so it's all a little anticlimactic."

She looked up at me and her face softened, "Oh, dear. What's going on with Zoey?"

"What?" I said, surprised at the change of topic.

"You're wearing your Zoey face. Is she coming home?"

"For a couple of days," I shrugged. "She called this morning."

Diane sighed. "Don't suppose it's about money."

I shook my head.

"Damn, another broken heart then." She took a sip of her cosmo. "I have to say, as much as I wanted a girl, I'm so glad I have boys. They'd rather die than talk to me about their love lives. They go straight to Mark. He, of course, then comes to me. But it's filtered, thank God."

Diane's boys were a study in contrasts. Devon was simply brilliant, the family overachiever, at Yale on scholarship. Ethan, a high school senior, was trying for a football scholarship because his grades were, horror of horrors, only Bs! We once hoped that Devon and Zoey would fall madly in love and make us in-laws but it was not to be, despite our best efforts and the fact that he's a couple of years younger. Devon thought my Zoey was a flake and she thought he was a snobby geek. What can you do?

"She's a good kid."

I knew it sounded defensive but every time I think about my beautiful girl, I am amazed. Her dad was a big, bulky guy with a buzz cut, and her mom, well, let's just say I've never turned heads when I walk down the street—or graced a magazine cover.

Our baby girl got his dark brown hair, which apparently tended to be wavy. When I once asked him if his hair was wavy, he looked at me like I was nuts since he hadn't seen it more than half an inch long since high school. She had my fair skin and green eyes, somehow bigger and more luminous than those behind my ever-present glasses. And I hate to brag, but she was not only prom queen, but also valedictorian of her class.

Diane placed her hand over mine across the table and gave it a pat as I came back to the conversation. "Of course she is. She'll find the right guy." She chuckled. "You have those hearts shooting out of your eyes again like the cartoon characters."

"She's only 24. She's not ready for a serious relationship but she thinks she is. I wish she'd finish her doctorate before settling down."

"Excuse me for pointing out the obvious, but when you and I were her age we were already married."

"Yes, but Harry was being deployed and we had no idea how long he'd be away …"

"… and Mark and I had promised ourselves that we'd wait until we graduated. I still don't think our parents ever knew we were living together in college."

A shadow crossed her face. "Lord, I hadn't thought about that in ages. Remember when I had that pregnancy scare and I thought we'd messed everything up? Neither of us breathed until I got my period." She swallowed. "You were the only one who knew that at the time."

I reached for her hand. "I was so worried for you. Maybe seeing you go through that was part of the reason we decided to wait to have kids until Harry could request permanent orders stateside."

Diane was lost in her reminiscing now. "And, after all that, who knew it would be so hard for us to start a family?"

It was time for me to get her mind off the fact that she had suffered two miscarriages before finally giving birth to Devon shortly before her thirtieth birthday. She still mourned those lost babies; some things you simply never get over.

"Okay, I surrender. I guess Zoey isn't too old to have a serious relationship, but things are different now than they were when we were young. And we both knew our husbands for years before we finally married."

She smiled and I knew she was back with me. "Well, you need to stop worrying and let her live her own life. And then, before you know it, you'll be a grandma!"

She loved to push that button. My stone-faced stare just wasn't enough. "You first!"

"Touché!" She picked up her menu. "Let's order and then I want all the juicy bits about Judy."

"Why do you always look at the menu and then order the Chicken Caesar?" I teased. She had it coming.

"There might be a new special. You never know."

"Right. Like that'll happen."

At that moment, Lizzie, with her impeccable timing, showed up with her pad. "Hi, Miranda. Are we having the usual today?"

I nodded. She turned to Diane, who was pretending to look thoughtfully at the menu. After a few long seconds, she shrugged. "Okay, that's fine. I'll have the Chicken Caesar salad, too." She pointed to her glass.

"Another round?"

Lizzie has been here forever. She knows the locals by name, drink preference and menu favorite, and she never forgets a face. She also has a way of making visitors to our small town feel at home. She's practically a local institution all by herself. I gave her a smile and she went off to get the drinks.

Diane leaned toward me. "So someone broke into Judy's house but didn't take anything?"

"Yep!" I took a sip of my drink and lowered my voice. "They didn't take anything, but they tore apart her antique trapunto skirt."

"That's the green thing with the puffy design that was in the calendar your guild put together last year?"

"Exactly!"

"Geez, that just seems ... mean." She pondered. "Who on earth would be that ticked off at Judy? I don't' know here that well but she seems like a nice person."

I was almost out of suspects myself but then I remembered one who was still not cleared. "Well, Susan Duncan is pretty irritated with her. You know her?"

"Sure, Mark sold Aaron and Susan their house on Maple Street." She added thoughtfully, "It was terrible last year when Aaron died so suddenly. I went over a few days later to pay my condolences and Susan looked like a ghost. She was absolutely in shock for weeks."

"Well, she marched into the drugstore last week and confronted Judy in front of customers. It got pretty nasty."

"Wait. I did hear about that! You know Jim and Mary Marshall live next door to me. Mary often stops over for coffee in the morning if I'm home. She said that Jim's mother was really upset about Susan's outburst and he had to stay with her for a while to calm her down. What on earth was that about?"

"Seems that Tommy was named starting pitcher for the high school team instead of Aidan and Susan was really teed off."

"Okaayy, that's it? That's completely out of character for Susan, isn't it?" Her brow furrowed. "Wait a minute, hold on. Susan was at the dance with us. She volunteered to help with the food. Aidan was there with Lori Clarke. I supposed it was her way of keeping an eye on him. I know she was there the whole time because after the band packed up and left, she was still there packing up leftovers and cleaning the food tables. She gave me a bag of cookies to take home. I'm fairly sure that Judy left before she did." She pointed a finger at me. "*And* I remember seeing Judy and Susan talking at one point. No one was throwing any punches anyway, so they must have reached a truce."

"Well, so much for that suspect." I took a swig of my cosmo.

At that moment, Lizzie appeared with our food and we crunched and munched contentedly. When we were more than half done and willing to speak again, I took up the conversation where we'd left it.

"We were talking about this at Quilt Guild last Saturday and, afterward the Moore twins reminded me that Laura Jenkins had a crush on Tom Smythin since grade school. They also said that she never married. And, get this; she submitted an old antique quilt for the calendar that was rejected. And, of course, Judy's skirt was accepted."

"No way! I'm telling you right now, I know Laura and she'd never do anything that vindictive. Tom may have broken her heart, but I don't see her breaking into his house all these years later." We'd finished eating and Diane drained her glass.

"Yeah, I know, it was pretty weak. But it seems she sprained her ankle two weeks ago and it's a pretty bad sprain. She's on crutches."

At that moment, Lizzie returned to the table to clear our dishes.

"Lizzie, could I get a glass of water, please?"

"Me, too!" Diane added.

"Sure thing, gals, I'll be right back."

Diane eyed me suspiciously. "Okay, give. You have something else on your mind?"

"I wouldn't say this to anyone else." I tried to find my words. "I can't help wondering if this is connected to the Haddon family. Taylor Perryman, Judy's cousin, has a lovely bed jacket that she inherited." I took a drink of the cold water Lizzie had just plunked down in front of both of us.

"If someone already damaged Judy's skirt, will they go after Taylor's bed jacket next? What if they break into her house? But what if I say something and get her all worried for nothing?" I paused. "And her jacket was on the calendar, too. So what if this is a calendar thing?"

"Hmm." That's one thing I love about Diane, she doesn't dismiss my wild and crazy thinking without giving it a chance.

Lizzie slid our check onto the edge of the table. "Anything else I can get you ladies?"

"No, we're all set. Thanks, Lizzie."

"Have a good one."

We waited until she walked away. Then Diane reacted to what I'd said. "Okay, I hate to add to your questions rather than help with the answers but ..."

I looked at her curiously.

"You're slipping, Miranda." She leaned forward and waved a finger at me. "How did the thief, or whoever did this, know enough to break in on the one night when no one was home?"

My mouth opened.

She ticked off on her fingers. "Judy was chaperoning Tommy and Ethan's prom. Judy told me that Jessie, who comes home most weekends, decided to stay at school to study for a test. And Tom was off on his annual boy's weekend with Mark and Ernie Phillips, right?"

She waved her hand like a magic wand. "And how often is her house empty until almost midnight or after? Same as yours or mine, like never!"

"Oh, Diane!" I had goose bumps.

She lowered her voice. "Somebody did their homework."

"Or somebody was watching the house," I whispered back, feeling suddenly sick. "Oh, wait! I had one other suspect: Sam Marconi, who works at the bank. Tom was recently promoted over him and he's been there longer. Or his wife, if she was mad about it."

"No way! Sam and Janet are deacons in our church. He doesn't have a mean bone in his body. He's been working at the bank since high school and he took some courses. But Janet told me he liked being head teller because there's less stress than in management. She told me how happy they were for Tom and they'd invited Tom and Judy out to dinner to celebrate the promotion. So you can cross him off your list for sure."

I sighed. "Already did. They were out of town celebrating their wedding anniversary with a long weekend in the Poconos."

She nodded and then added thoughtfully, "Well, we may not have any good suspects but there's one more thing we do know. This miserable piece of crap didn't want to run into anyone, so they're clearly not looking to hurt anybody."

I looked at my watch. "Shoot, I've gotta go get ready for the kid. I took the afternoon off to do some cleaning and laundry that I usually do on Saturdays. She'll be here in a few hours."

"Call me," she ordered as we put our money down on the check.

I slid out of the booth and placed a hand on her shoulder. "Thanks, sweetie."

She laughed. "For what, making it worse?"

"No, for being my friend!"

She gave me a hug. "You, Sherlock, may call me Watson." She finished with a rather impressive eyebrow wiggle.

Chapter Fourteen

"Come on, Mom. Let's get dressed up and go out someplace different." Zoey bounced up and down on her toes, a habit I've been trying to break for almost 24 years.

I thought for a second. "There's a new seafood place across town by the Holiday Inn Express. I think it's called Seafood Palace or something grand like that."

"Excellent."

We both giggled when, an hour later, we walked into the restaurant. Palace seemed to be the decorating scheme as well as the name. It was so far over the top that we both had all we could do to remain straight-faced while we were seated. It was hilarious. Red and gold colors dominated, with serious tassels and fringe. We were seated by the window, overlooking the river, which gave our eyes some relief. We didn't look at each other until we had composed ourselves.

Our waiter's uniform was slightly lower key with black pants and short red jacket over a white shirt and black bowtie. We settled in with a shrimp appetizer and a glass of zinfandel. I always have to remind myself, watching Zoey sip hers, that she's old enough to drink.

She looked at me and grinned. "Stop it."

I raised an eyebrow. "What?"

"You're surprised—again—that I'm old enough to drink." She patted my hand. "I have been for a while now, Mom." Her lovely eyes darkened. "I'm old enough for a lot of stuff."

I nodded. "And some of it hurts." I paused for a second, "I read somewhere recently that falling in love is wonderful and falling out of love is truly terrible, but it's not the end of the world. Sometimes it's hard to remember that."

She raised an eyebrow in an exact imitation of what I had done. "How did you know?"

"Mother's intuition! So no more Tony?"

She sighed in exasperation. "Tony was last year, Mom. This is Michael." I could see her eyes glistening. "I really thought he was the one."

Sometimes silence is the better part of mothering. I waited for the gush of angst I knew would follow.

One of her friends had seen Michael having dinner with a lovely redhead. They seemed pretty cozy and it didn't look like business to her. She had called Zoey, saying, "I hate to be the one to tell you this …!" Sure she did! Michael had never mentioned this dinner to Zoey.

She was deeply wounded, humiliated, and I believe, surprised. Zoey dumps guys; they don't dump her. At last she had learned the lesson a less attractive girl would have learned in high school, as I had. My heart still ached for her.

She looked to me for words of wisdom and guidance. Without giving much thought to it, I merely stated, "Life sucks!"

Perhaps because my answer was so unexpected, she burst out laughing. Her buoyant laughter rang through the half-filled restaurant and I couldn't help but join her. Then she wiped her eyes on her napkin, not from tears of pain but of laughter, and my work here was done.

Finally, she responded. "Gee, thanks, Mom. You always know just the right thing to say."

And that set us both off again.

We were finishing our cheesecake and coffee, seafood restaurants not generally being known for their variety of dessert choices, when her head swiveled to the entrance and back. She leaned toward me. "Mom, do you see the woman coming in right now? Don't stare."

110

I tried to sneak an unobtrusive peek. "Okay. Red dress. Blonde helmet hair. Built like a ..."

"That's her. I'll tell you later."

As we drove home, she gave me the details. "I'm sure that was Dr. Moriarty. Do you remember when I told you that I monitored a guest lecture by an expert in antique textiles from the university?"

"Whoa, back it up. So she's Professor Moriarty?" I chortled.

She joined me. "I know. That's why she prefers to be called 'Doctor.' Can you imagine going through that all day long? I swear to God I'd change my name." She took a breath. "Here's the thing. She's a big deal in Boston and New York. What on earth is she doing in Cutler, Pennsylvania?"

What, indeed, especially wearing a large black hat and sunglasses indoors, trying to be inconspicuous in a way that made her ridiculously conspicuous.

As we were leaving, I noticed that she was sitting with Dan Mayers from the *Cutler Chronicle*. The young reporter had given us some good publicity for the calendar. They were chatting comfortably.

Of course, my mystery-loving mind kicked in. Dan would be an invaluable and, most likely, innocent source for information about the locals now, wouldn't he? Let's just say it was suspicious. And, after all, I had no suspects left and her name was Moriarty.

It was wonderful to wake up to the smell of coffee already brewing. Zoey handed me a mug and returned to the eggs she was scrambling. Neither of us was a gourmet chef but I had made sure she knew enough to be able to feed herself when she left home. We munched through breakfast, me quiet and thinking, as usual, and she monitoring her cellphone every minute, as usual.

"What are you planning to do today?" I finally ventured.

"I think I'll take it easy, maybe read a good book." She grinned at me.

I had been encouraging her to read since she was, well, three. I could have pointed out that she wouldn't be finishing her doctorate without my encouragement in her formative years, but sometimes stating the obvious is not the right choice.

"Funny girl! Well, I have my Quilt Guild this afternoon. But if you'd like to go shopping or something this morning."

Then something happened that had never happened before. She turned down a trip to the mall.

"No thanks, Mom. I'm good. But, if you'd like to walk around downtown and show me what's changed since my last visit, I think that might be fun."

"Incredibly, there are a few new shops that I don't think you've seen. Let's do that."

So we cleaned up our dishes and headed off. We stopped by the new wine shop, The Grapes of Grath, where Zoey and Vinnie engaged in a California vs. French wine discussion which she knew a bit too much about to suit me.

At the brand-new high-end lingerie shop down the street, Over's Unders, we introduced ourselves to the proprietress, a newcomer to town named Ellen Over. She showed Zoey several lacy camisole and bikini sets. I held my tongue but it wasn't easy.

When Ellen suggested that I try on a pale blue lace nightie, I felt Zoey's smile as she waited for my answer. I hated the fact that I went completely red-faced and stuttered, "Ah no, no thank you." I walked outside to wait for Zoey, who came out after a few minutes carrying a small shopping bag. I didn't ask.

Then there was the mandatory visit to Queenie's where Zoey exclaimed over all the designer fabrics and the displays of quilts and throws. I say mandatory because if Queenie found out that Zoey was in town and didn't stop by, I would have heard about it later and often.

We sauntered around town window-shopping and saying "Hello" to people we met on the street, and then went to lunch at Zoey's favorite spot, Tex's Tacos. That's where we parted ways. She said she might go home and take a nap because she hadn't slept well, and I headed back to Queenie's.

Judy's skirt had been there for a few days so it was already well on its way when Queenie showed it to us. She had done an amazing job and it looked very much like it had before. We all cheered her for the effort.

All that was needed was to handstitch a few long seams and reattach the waistband. Our best seamstresses, Sarah and Harriet, offered to finish up. Judy was deeply touched and hesitantly asked if she could pay for the repairs.

Queenie looked momentarily offended but then her face brightened. "How about coming with me to St. John's someday instead?"

We all knew that Queenie spent one day a week at the soup kitchen there. Judy said she'd love to do that. And the issue was cheerfully resolved.

It was Brittany who finally asked the question on the tip of all of our tongues. "We still have no idea why anyone tore the skirt, right?"

"No, we don't," I put in quickly.

After the group, Gabe, who had been quiet through the whole meeting, caught up to me as I got to my car. I still suspected that he knew more about the break-in at Judy's than he was saying and had no idea why he'd come to my house. I had spent an hour or two trying to convince myself that he liked me; that it wasn't just to throw me off the track of wondering what he was up to.

"Miranda!"

I stopped just as I was about to open my car door and turned to lean against it.

"Hey, Gabe! What's up?"

He smiled. "I had a great time the other night. And I was, uh, wondering if we could have dinner."

I sighed with relief, sort of. He wouldn't be much of a thief or quilt ripper if he … oh, but wait, yes, he could. Years of watching British mysteries might have rendered me a bit cynical by nature.

There was also the fact that I had so far proven, rather obviously, resistible to the local single men of my age bracket. I processed quickly. I could play this game and reverse it to find out what he knew.

"It was fun to have someone to beat, other than Harry." I teased.

I watched his shoulders relax a bit. Librarians and amateur sleuths notice things like that.

"I suppose tonight would be out of the question?"

"My daughter's in town. I'm sorry."

"Maybe tomorrow night?"

I had to admit it had been a while since anyone had been so desperate for a date with me. "Can I let you know? I never have any idea how long she's staying …"

"… or what she needs from her mother?" he finished with a grin.

"Exactly. Thanks for understanding."

If I had waited another hour, my answer might have been different. When I got home, Zoey was on her phone, sounding more upbeat than she had before. She clicked off and ran over and hugged me.

"Good news?"

"Oh, Mom, that was Michael. He swears he didn't cheat on me. The girl was a friend from college and she was only in Boston that one evening. So he had dinner with her but that was all. He feels awful. He didn't tell me because he didn't want me to get the wrong impression. He knows now that he should have told me the truth upfront. He wants me to come back so we can talk it out."

I felt a knot forming in the pit of my stomach. "And you're going?"

Something in my tone made her step back. "Don't you think I should?"

"Oh, honey, I've never met the man. It's really not fair for me to even have an opinion."

"And yet I feel like you do."

I took a breath. "If he didn't tell you the truth about an innocent dinner with an old friend ..."

She swallowed hard but nodded.

"... can you truly trust him?"

"I hear what you're saying, Mom, I do," she said quietly. "But we're so good together. I think I'd like to give him another chance."

It was my turn to nod. If Harry had lied to me, even by omission, about spending time with another woman before we were married, I'm pretty sure I wouldn't have had the heart to try again. But Zoey wasn't me; it was her life. As much as I wanted to live it for her and spare her any pain, I couldn't.

"Okay, honey."

"I knew you'd understand." She bounced on her toes. "I'm going back to Boston as soon as I can get packed. You don't mind do you?"

"Of course not, this is your home. You come and go whenever you want. It's been great having you here."

She laid her hands on my shoulders. Being about five inches taller than me, she looked down into my eyes. "Mom, don't you think it's time you gave someone a chance yourself?"

I gave her my patented disgusted-mother look.

"I know, right, me giving you relationship advice. Weird, huh!" She giggled. "But seriously, it's been long enough. I hate the thought of you being alone in this house. I worry about you."

At that, I laughed out loud.

"I mean it. What happened with Jack?"

"Jack's been a friend for a long time. But he was Dad's friend, too." I shrugged. "We agreed that dating felt a little too weird. We're still friends."

She shook her head. "You need to try harder."

I grinned at her and a smile lit up her face. But she wagged a finger at me. "I mean it."

"Sure." I grabbed her finger and pulled her into a hug.

In less than an hour, she was gone. And the house felt emptier and quieter than it had before, I freely admit. Even Harry seemed to feel it. I found him napping on her bed and was tempted to join him.

Instead, I called Gabe to tell him I was actually free for dinner. "Hi, it's Miranda. Zoey has rushed off and I'm now free for dinner, if you're still free, that is," I added, feeling slightly stupid.

"I am and I'm delighted." He added, "Would you, uh, mind choosing the restaurant? I haven't eaten out much since

I've been here." He paused. "I guess I should say I've been taking most of my meals at Sylvia's Diner."

"You could do worse. She's a bit pushy but she's a great cook."

"Absolutely, but perhaps something just a bit more … upscale?"

I laughed and thought for a second, "Okay, how about the Webster Hotel's dining room. It's called Kelly's and they do a nice steak, even a decent fish. By fish, I mean salmon, of course, this being meat and potatoes country. You're not a vegetarian, are you?"

"Lord, no! A steak sounds great."

"That's good, because if you were vegetarian, you'd be just about out of luck around here. Your choices would be macaroni and cheese off the kid's menu, or a potato of some kind, and a choice between the ever-popular green beans or corn."

He laughed out loud. "A steak and baked potato, it is."

"I'll meet you there, if you don't mind. Let's say seven?"

"Perfect." He added, "See you then."

As soon as he disconnected the call from Miranda, Gabe dialed another number.

"It's me. I'm having dinner with the local librarian, the one I told you about who's already figured out Taylor Perryman is next. She's a member of the Quilt Guild and seems to be a bit of a mystery buff."

"I'm not clear on how you think this is going to help us."

"She's smart and I think I can gain valuable information on what the locals know and hopefully keep anyone from getting hurt. Our goal is to get Amy out of here quietly, and without getting the police involved, right?"

Dr. Moriarty thought it over. "Do you think this woman has any idea what's actually going on?"

"Not really. I think she's working on it and she certainly knows just about everyone in town." He hesitated. "I do know she's working on the calendar lead, but I'm not sure she's made the Haddon connection."

When she didn't respond, he added with mild irritation, "Have *you* made any progress?"

A sigh came through the phone. "I spoke to that local reporter again today and he's equally clueless. I suppose the cousin's the next logical step. I wish there was some way to get that family out of town for a day or two. I'm already sick of this burg."

"No one asked you to come."

She ignored that. "I have my contacts on the lookout back in Boston in case Amy shows up there. Only time will tell. Anyway, enjoy your dinner with the librarian and try not to be too clever, will you?"

His temper rose. "Remember who you're talking to, Doctor."

She chuckled. "My employee, I believe, the one who already let Amy get away once!" She hung up before he could respond.

The young reporter hadn't been very helpful and she had to be so careful what questions she asked. He'd hinted at an exclusive interview regarding her latest novel and she'd hinted that if he was useful in providing her some research information, she might be able to accommodate him. For that tidbit, he'd agreed to keep the fact that she was in town out of the paper until she was ready to do the interview.

This was a small town and the gossip mill was buzzing about the break-in at the Smythin house. She had heard it at the Donut Shoppe where she was downing her third cup of surpisingly decent dark roast coffee. She took a bite of the chocolate-covered, custard-filled donut then placed it on a napkin. Patricia was a large, curvaceous woman and, despite the extensive vocabulary that her work demanded, d-i-e-t was a four-letter word that she'd never used.

She felt a tad down. Why had she come? She gave herself an answer that felt odd. Sitting in her office in Boston, she missed Amy. Back at the apartment, she missed Amy. For the first time in years, Patricia Moriarty felt alone. But she had also put Downing in charge of finding the girl and she couldn't seem to control him. That made her angry and she had to take action. So she'd come to Cutler.

Chapter Fifteen

I was nervous. I'd been out on three "dates" in the past year. A *Jeopardy* challenge didn't really count, even by my modest standards.

Jack was one of Harry's friends and a widower. He'd invited me to dinner. We had a pleasant but awkward time. All we had in common was my dead husband and his dead wife. We agreed that we should keep in touch and we had, but he didn't ask me out again and that was a relief for both of us, I think. End of story.

Marshall was a book salesman who had stopped in the library and invited me to lunch. We talked over two hours about books and authors that we loved; we had so much in common. He told me about his travels around the world. Reading was his first love and travel was his second. We were having a great time until he mentioned his partner, Travis. End of story.

Then there was George, a widower, who missed his wife terribly. He was a regular at the library and loved to stop by my office to talk. And I mean talk.

One particular Friday as I was leaving for the day and about to lock the library front door, George came running toward the entrance.

"Wait, Miranda, wait!"

"Oh my gosh, George, I almost locked you in."

"I know and I'm so sorry." As he gasped for air, I waited. "I was reading in one of those soft leather chairs in the fiction room and dozed off. I woke up when I heard you near the door."

He caught his breath and laughed. "I don't know when I've moved that fast, although it wouldn't have been too bad to be locked in the library. I spend most of my time here anyway."

"Yes, you do." I looked at him closely. "George, are you all right?"

"Just a lonely old man, my dear."

I thought for a moment and realized that I was going home to an empty house, except for Harry, that is.

"Hey, George, how about we go down to Sylvia's and get a burger? Do you have any dinner plans?"

While we shared a couple of burgers and a huge plate of fries, I learned that George had two sons and a daughter in upstate New York. They had all invited him to come and stay after Mildred died. But George had declined, saying he needed his independence and didn't want to be a burden.

"Now I think I made the wrong decision. Everyone here has been very kind but I think I may be ready."

"Ready for what ...?" Alarms went off as a number of unpleasant options ran through my head.

"Ready to sell the house and move to my oldest son's place outside of Rochester. He has an extra room and bath that he's set up for me and it's only a few blocks from the local library."

Hallelujah! What a relief.

"Well, I'm glad you didn't make a hasty decision after Mildred passed." I patted his hand and smiled reassuringly. "Now you've had time to think about it. You should call your son, and soon. I'm sure he can help you wrap up things here, and your house is wonderful. It should sell quickly."

Relief flashed across his dear old wrinkled face. "Yes, I know you're right. It's been in the family for years and we've always taken good care of it. I even had a few calls from real estate people after Mildred passed, but that just made me mad. Vultures!"

"Well, I would definitely not be listing with them. But there are some great realtors in town who would love to list your house." I gave him Mark's name and number, putting an end to that story as well.

So that's the extent of my dating life over the past year. But tonight felt different. Gabe is tall, distinguished-looking, and appears to be in good physical shape. He has short white hair, although I don't think he's much older than me, and crystal blue eyes (think *Mission Impossible*'s Peter Graves from the '60s TV show). He has an easy smile and his mouth crinkles at the corners when he's trying not to laugh. He has good hands; I notice things like that. My Harry had huge, hardworking hands. It's a quirk, I'm sure, but I don't think I could be interested in a man with small hands. Gabe's hands are a good size and firm and strong. When I'm being held, or touched, I want to feel like I'm really being held or touched, if you know what I mean. Not that I've thought about his hands a lot. *Okay, moving on.*

He's an attractive man and I had butterflies in my stomach thinking about what might happen.

I stood before the full-length mirror in my bedroom and tried on the dresses that still fit. I must admit, that I rarely wear dresses, well actually never. They're just not practical at work.

Back to my closet: Red, too pushy! White, no way!

Number three, not too bad! I'd bought this dress a few years ago because I loved it, but hadn't had a reason to wear it. It's a pale floral that looks almost like watercolors: mostly green, blue, and lilac in muted tones on a cream background.

I turned slightly and spoke to my reflection. "Not bad for a 52-year-old, slightly overweight librarian."

I'd let my shoulder-length hair down from its usual ponytail or topknot that I wear to the library. I even went for a bit of makeup and lipstick, also things I don't do on a daily basis.

Last step was to put on my two-inch cream-colored heels that again I almost never wear. I grabbed a lightweight lilac scarf that could work as a shawl because, for some reason, most restaurants keep their air conditioners down really low. I guess they want us to eat and pay and leave as quickly as possible. No chance of lingering over a meal when you're shivering!

But now I had to get moving or I'd be late for my date. Why were my knees shaking? I tried to relax by taking myself to a happy place in my mind.

When I arrived at Kelly's, Gabe was seated at the corner table at the back of the restaurant, much to my relief. I prefer corner tables when I can get one. I don't need to watch the door like an old west poker player. It's the noise! I prefer to have a deflecting wall behind me. And cellphones are the curse of civilized dining as far as I'm concerned.

He gave me a wave, as if that shock of white hair was hard to see in the subtle lighting of the half-filled restaurant.

"I can see why you chose this place." He stood and held my chair.

"As I said, the food's pretty good and it's fairly quiet." I returned his quiet smile.

"And none of your friends are likely to see us here." A touch of mischief twinkled across his tanned face.

I felt my cheeks color but I wasn't going to lie so I babbled, "True. I don't know why it would matter, really. It's just that this town has a gossip grapevine that is not to be believed."

"I figured that out already." He touched my hand. "It's fine, really. I was teasing you."

"I know it's ridiculous. I'm single, you're single." I paused. "You are single, right?"

"Yes. Divorced, actually."

"I'm sorry."

He shrugged. "I've adjusted. It took a while. It sounds absurd now, but it caught me by surprise. I didn't realize I was a bad husband, and for over twenty-five years, apparently."

That hit a bit of a nerve with me. It's a story I've heard before and, frankly, I find it hard to believe that one partner can be so unhappy that they need to leave and the other has no clue? How can someone hide their discontent over a long period of time? Obviously, someone isn't paying attention.

Thank God the waiter came over before I put my size seven in my mouth.

"Our featured appetizer is the bruschetta with fresh tomato and a bite of prosciutto. The salad this evening is a mix of country greens with grapes, walnuts, and Boursin cheese. The entrée special this evening is beef bourguignon prepared with a pinot noir and served on sourdough toast. We also have the salmon grilled with a caper-and-mustard sauce. I will be happy to suggest a wine as well."

My mouth was watering as he spoke. Gabe and I exchanged glances.

"That sounds good." He grinned.

I chuckled and even the waiter, who had been focused on his spiel, smiled.

"Tough decision. Okay, I'm going with the salad and the beef bourguignon." Then I relaxed, one decision made.

"Sounds great, but let's have the bruschetta as well." He hesitated, and then looked at the waiter. "I'm thinking we might as well have a bottle of pinot noir to go with the entrée?"

The waited nodded his approval and departed.

When he left the table, we started over. I dipped into my limited supply of casual conversation subjects. "I was going to start with the ever-popular 'Tell me about yourself,' but I think we've crossed that bridge already."

He smiled. "What would you like to know now that we've agreed I'm single?"

"Well, you know that I have a daughter. Do you have any kids?"

"A son, Kevin. He's 26 and is currently in Seattle, trying to find himself."

The slightly disgruntled look on his face made me smile and I couldn't resist. "Has he tried looking in the mirror?"

"That's exactly what I told him!" He laughed and then shrugged. "Kids, huh? So your little birdie flew home and then off again?"

I nodded. "Seems like they only need to make sure the nest is still there sometimes."

His face took on a pensive look. "Maybe when we have only the one, we focus on them too much."

"That seems highly probable." I moved on. "So tell me about you. Where are you from? What do you do? And how on earth did you land in Cutler?"

"I was born in Natick, Massachusetts. And ..." He leaned forward and lowered his voice. "I worked for the government."

"Really?" Aha! My *Jeopardy* info confirmed. I leaned forward too. "Doing what? And don't even think of saying that if you told me, you'd have to kill me."

He smiled, "More like bore you to tears, I'm afraid. At any rate, I took early retirement as soon as I could. And to complete your background check, I'm 57. I'm taking some time to travel and explore the country and I happened upon Cutler and decided to stay awhile."

I tried to disguise my lack of belief. In all my life, no one had ever wandered into Cutler. Of course there was Andy but he was a special case.

"I guess I can see the draw of moving someplace new." I answered politely. "And I don't know where that came from since I was born and raised here and have never even thought about doing anything like that." I paused. "I would like to travel, I think."

"Well, who knows, maybe you will one day."

"I guess only time will tell." I met his eyes, and then looked away.

He let me off the hook gently. "Now I think it's your turn to tell me your life story."

There was something about those blue eyes that made me feel safe.

"Not much to tell, I'm afraid. I married Harry Hathaway right after college and we have a daughter, Zoey. Harry was a couple of years older than me. He did 30 years in the Marine Corps before he retired.

"After a few tours overseas, Harry was stationed at Quantico where he trained officers in close contact combat techniques. We were able to stay here and he traveled back and forth but mostly spent three months there and then a month here. He loved hunting and fishing and, thank God, was very handy around the house. Over the years, he remodeled most of our house.

"We always figured that once we got Zoey through college, I would retire and we'd travel together. Then she decided to go on for her master's and we made plans. Then she decided to get her doctorate and we made more plans." I took a sip of my water.

"You don't have to talk about it, if you don't want to."

"No, it's fine. It's been almost two years now." I took a deep breath.

"Harry was an expert hunter and so was, or is, his best friend, Bill Johnson. They were deer hunting and, well, Harry didn't make it home. I never wanted to know the details." I took another sip of the cold drink. "Poor Bill." I sighed.

"I'm so sorry."

I blinked myself back to the conversation. I took a piece of bread from the basket and tried to throw the line out there casually. "I have to believe there's a reason he's gone and I'm still here."

Gabe didn't respond and I took a bite of bread before meeting that blue gaze. It showed the compassion and understanding that only comes from painful experience. It was obvious that his divorce had taken its toll.

We really needed to lighten up so I switched gears. "So how on earth did you learn to quilt?"

He took up the change of subject gratefully. "My wife had gotten into it before the divorce, and when she brought in the long-arm quilting machine it got my attention." He paused and his face stiffened.

"I had been made aware that I didn't take an interest in anything she did. So when she was learning how to operate the monstrosity, I read the manual and stepped in. I found out I was actually better at it than she was. She would put the quilts together and I would do the machine quilting. I enjoyed it! It was a great tension reliever for me because it was so different from my day job."

He grinned at me ruefully. "She had offered me the choice between quilting and yoga. And, ironically, it seems I made the wrong choice. She left me for her yoga instructor."

The food arrived at that opportune moment.

Despite the sadness of this first exchange, we ate in comfortable silence, knowing each other better than we had when we took our seats. When the waiter returned to take our dessert orders, I recommended the apple pie which was their specialty. We ordered two of those served warm and topped with vanilla ice cream, of course.

Finally, Gabe asked about Judy's break-in.

I knew that the best way to get information was to give a little. So I told him that Judy was thinking of donating the skirt to a museum. She had inherited it as part of the Haddon family legacy from the Revolutionary War period.

"Wow. That's really interesting. It's hard to wrap your head around holding clothing that someone may have worn during the 1700s and that has survived this long."

"Absolutely. The skirt is a beautiful piece. It does have value in its age and origin. But what makes this break-in all the more puzzling is that the person took it apart. They didn't take it or destroy it completely."

He took a bite of his pie before commenting. "Ah, but I have a feeling you have a theory."

"Not really." How far should I go? I didn't like the idea of giving something for nothing. So I stuck with what I was sure he already knew.

"The only thing that concerns us is that this might have something to do with the Quilt Guild's calendar. You remember Brittany mentioning it when Queenie told us what had happened."

He nodded. "Sure. So … are you thinking that someone is going to go after the other items shown on the calendar?

Why would they do that? This skirt would only have historical value if it were whole. And even then, any expert would have a lot of questions and certainly confirm its provenance."

"It's just a thought, I guess." I paused. "I'd hate to think that we might have set those people up for robbery because they were kind enough to share their pieces for our calendar." I shook my head in frustration. "Especially since the proceeds go to local charities. So tell me, what do you think?"

"I haven't been here long enough to know Judy and her family very well but she hardly seems the kind of woman to have enemies. And why wouldn't they have destroyed her entire quilting room, hell—excuse me—her whole house if they were that pissed—excuse me—off?"

I waved off his apologies with a flick of my hand. "You don't need to apologize. Harry was a Marine, remember, and he had quite a mouth on him so I automatically filter out bad words! But because I'm often surrounded by children at the library, I try really hard not to swear. And you're right, of course. It does appear to be specifically targeted."

"But nothing was taken, she's sure?" He looked to me for confirmation.

"She says not."

"Do you mind if I take your speculation forward a bit?"

"Please do. I've got nothing."

He breathed out slowly. "Let's say that the calendar drew someone's attention to the Haddon family heirlooms. They were clearly the oldest pieces on that calendar."

I interrupted. "The Quilt Ripper."

"What?"

"That's what I call the … perp, The Quilt Ripper."

A smile played at the corners of his mouth but he had the discretion to stifle it. "Okay, so the ... Quilt Ripper sees Judy's skirt on the calendar, reads that it's a Haddon family heirloom, and, for God knows what reason, tears it apart." His voice had become quite serious. "I understand that Officer Perryman—"

"He prefers Chief Perryman," I interrupted again then apologized. "Sorry, please go on."

He bowed his head graciously. "Chief Perryman's wife, Taylor, is Judy's cousin. And she has an item on the calendar, does she not?"

I allowed my eyes to widen, trying not to give away that I'd already thought of that. Queenie would have been proud of my performance.

"Of course, it's a blue bed jacket. Do you really think the Quilt Ripper is going to go after it next?"

"I have no idea. But then there wouldn't be much opportunity, would there? Since he's the Chief of Police, I don't imagine he takes weekends off or anything."

"No, but everyone knows his hours. And Taylor goes to see her brother in Pittsburgh every month or so. He has some kind of cancer, I think. I forget exactly what." I allowed a sudden realization to flicker over my face.

"What is it? Have you thought of something?"

I certainly had his full attention now. "It's just that I think Taylor's going to Pittsburgh next Friday!" I swallowed. "But surely no one would be dumb enough to break into a policeman's house? Would they?"

He shrugged. "Probably not. Let's just hope this person has gone away and empty-handed to boot." He signaled for the check.

As we walked out, he said softly. "Thank you, Miranda. I don't know when I last enjoyed a meal this much."

"The food was actually better than I expected."

"I wasn't talking about just the food." He chuckled.

"Next time I'll take you to the Seafood Palace. Now that's an experience to remember!" I teased.

He said nothing.

I couldn't for the life of me figure out what to say next so I kept my mouth shut.

At my car door, he leaned down and pecked my cheek. "Good night, Miranda."

"Good night," I managed. After I was safely in my car, I choked down the lump in my throat and drove home.

When I arrived, no one waited by the door, as usual.

"Harry, where are you?" I called out but received no answer.

I walked to the living room and he was on his chair, pretending to be asleep.

"Okay, buster, that's quite enough 'attitude' from you. I need to talk and you'd better listen up."

He didn't move and faked a snore.

I was annoyed by the tears on my cheeks. "I think I screwed up. Clearly, I suck at this dating thing so badly I will most likely never get a second chance with anyone. I've got some nerve trying to give Zoey advice in the love department because I am obviously clueless," I ranted.

I marched to the kitchen and poured myself a glass of wine before returning to my chair. Yes, I know I was over my two-glass limit but these were extenuating circumstances!

Harry had turned over onto his back with paws in the air, squeezing his eyes shut, clearly showing his disinterest in anything I had to say, but I continued anyway.

"He didn't say, 'I'll give you a call' or 'We should do this again.' But I went right ahead and told him I'd take him to the Seafood Palace next time. Ohmigod, he probably thinks I'm some desperate widow woman just trying to get laid. What's wrong with me? Why am I so upset?"

I got nothing but an ear flicker.

I moved from embarrassed to teed off. "Well, even if he does ask me out again, I'm not sure I'll go. I'm not sure I want to be dating someone from my Quilt Guild. This is definitely gonna be awkward."

Harry jumped to the floor, clearly indicating that he was bored with this discussion, and walked out, heading to bed.

"Great! Rejected by two men in one night!" I called out to the retreating tail.

I drained my wine glass and turned out the lights.

Chapter Sixteen

Next stop: Allenville, a suburb of Boston. It took a little over an hour to get there and locate the Haddon Jeffers house. It was a beautiful stone house in an affluent, upscale community. The good news was that each house had a fairly large lot and the houses were spread out. That was both good and bad for Amy.

The house was in one of those neighborhoods with private security services. She simply couldn't park anywhere near the house without having a patrol pull up within fifteen minutes. You either belonged there or you didn't, and her rented silver Honda clearly didn't. A blue "Sullivan Security" car with two rent-a-cops in it cruised past her twice in the short time she was there.

She had to be creative and look seriously nonthreatening. She went back to town, checked into a hotel, and rented a bicycle.

Her Internet research had shown that Constance Haddon Jeffers and her husband, Edward, lived in the house. They had one daughter, who was a graduate student at Boston University, but she commuted and was home several days a week. Even knowing that, she'd have to take the time to confirm the family's schedules and, in this neighborhood, watch out for the maid.

The next morning, Amy rode her rented bicycle past the house and waved cheerfully to the security guards in their small blue cars. There was a beat-up gray Ford in the driveway. Maid?

The second day, she cruised by in the early afternoon and the security guard returned her wave. No gray car.

It took her a week to figure out the regular comings and goings. The maid came on Monday and Thursday. They must have a pool in back because a service showed up on Wednesday. The trash was picked up on Friday. She kept an eye out for a lawn maintenance guy. But he didn't show.

She took the weekend off. There was bound to be more people around and it was too big a risk that she might be seen. On Monday, she rode by and noted the Ford there again.

Finally, on the second Tuesday, a kid in a pickup truck turned into the driveway and went into the garage. Amy knew that no one else was in the house.

Shortly thereafter, he put up the garage door and come out on a riding mower, which he parked in the driveway and went back in. After dragging out a push mower, he carried out a trimmer and placed them in the driveway as well. He jumped on the rider and went around the house to the back yard and started mowing. With the driveway not visible from the other houses and the kid mowing out back, this was the chance she'd been waiting for.

Amy quickly made her way up the drive and went into the garage. As she expected, there was a door between the garage and short entryway into the house. God forbid the homeowners should have to get wet going from car to house! An expert on a TV show she had seen had said that even folks who thought their home was totally secure never locked this door. It had taken him less than a minute to enter a secure house by taking the garage door opener out of an unlocked car in the driveway and entering through the garage into the house. Useful. Just like that, she was in. She stood still and waited for the alarm to go off. When it didn't, she moved quickly through the first floor, room by room, making sure she could still hear the mower.

She found what she was looking for upstairs in the guest room! She breathed out slowly as she touched the old wooden trunk reverently. Slowly, she raised the lid and found that it was full of antique quilts.

The mower stopped humming. She peeked out the window and waited. The boy came back around the house with the trimmer and started it up. Hurry! She lifted out the quilts and put them on the bed. Then she pulled out her Swiss army knife and used the handle to tap the back wall of the trunk. *Tap, tap, tap, clink.* A hollow sound. She did it again. She took her flashlight and looked carefully at the framing.

She had studied Chinese puzzle constructions enough to know that you had to pull one side and push the other at the same time. There were four supports. It took her three tries to line them up before the back center board fell down about three inches. Amy reached into the hollow and pulled out two pouches of coins. Her heart was beating so loudly she could hear it in her ears. It was all she could do to keep from shouting in victory.

But she made herself stop and listen for the high-pitched squeal of the trimmer, and then stuffed the pouches into her pockets. She forced herself to move slowly down the stairs, into the garage, and down the driveway.

When she was safely holding her bike handles, she breathed. The boy was back on the mower with his iPod earbuds in and was oblivious to anyone or anything other than making a nice neat pattern in the cut grass.

Her heart was still beating like a drum in her ears; her pulse raced. What if someone noticed that the trunk had been opened? What if they had security cameras trained on the driveway? Suddenly, she panicked. Had she put the quilts back?

She took a drink from her water bottle and closed her eyes. *Calm down.* They might never notice. It was a guest room. The maid would come on Thursday and probably just put them back; thinking someone in the household had been looking for something.

When her wobbly legs were finally able to pedal, she slowly made her way back to town.

Amy went to her motel room and emptied the coin pouches onto the spare bed. She examined them, sorted them, and then counted. There were 62 pieces in all. She recognized the pound, guinea, and shilling coins, and knew that they were made of gold and silver. At today's rates, this had to be a small fortune. She took the strand of pearls from the velvet pouch she'd put them in and the sapphire earrings from another.

She couldn't believe it! She lay back on her pillow and smiled for a while. It was real. She was holding the Haddon heirlooms in her hands. And nobody even knew they existed.

Chapter Seventeen

"Mom!"

I clutched my morning coffee close and braced for the next chapter of the ongoing saga that was Zoey's love life.

"Hi, honey."

"You're not gonna believe this!"

Oh, I bet I will, I thought to myself. Although she sounded pretty upbeat if she was going to tell me Michael screwed up again.

"Okaayy," I ventured.

"I ran into Ellie Sherman, who has a friend who knows Annie Haddon Jeffers. She goes here too."

I perked up. "*Haddon* Jeffers?"

"*I know!* Here's the scoop. Annie's mom is one of the Haddon cousins, just like Judy at the quilt club."

"Whoa." I was torn between relief that Zoey didn't seem to be in crisis mode and concern that there were more Haddons out there.

"Right. So she told me that Annie's house was broken into ..." She paused for effect, and then giggled. "Drum roll, please. There was an old oak trunk that was brought over on a ship during the Revolutionary War era by a relative. Now get this, it was taken apart but not stolen!"

I gasped, and it wasn't just because I was being polite. "Oh no!"

She was still excited. "So you were right, Mom. There's definitely something creepy going on."

I thought hard and fast. "Honey, I don't suppose there's a local police report or anything in writing about this?"

Her laughter trickled through the phone. "I knew you'd ask me for corroboration. I know you so well. And it made the police blotter in their local newspaper, the *Allenville Register*. Ellie got her friend to track it down and I had her send me a copy."

"This is amazing. Can you …"

"I already did. I sent you an email earlier. You know, Mom, you have to get a smart phone, seriously, and look at it all the time. You have to keep up."

It was my turn to laugh. I wasn't sure I really wanted to be chained to a phone and in constant contact with anyone at any time. Not exactly a Luddite but maybe a wannabe.

"I know, dear, maybe one of these days. But thank you so much, Zoey. I have no idea what this means but it sure means something."

"And the plot thickens," she said in a deep stage voice. "Well, gotta run, Mom. Michael's meeting me for breakfast and I'm already late. Talk to you later."

"Okay, love." I paused, biting back the maternal words of wisdom. "Zoey …"

"I know, Mom," she said soberly. "But everyone is entitled to one mistake. We're taking it slow and careful this time. I won't settle for anything but total honesty. He gets that now."

I smiled into my old-fashioned basic flip phone. "I love you, you goofy girl."

"Back at ya. Let me know what happens next." And she clicked off.

I dashed into my office, which is just off the kitchen, and turned on my desktop computer. After refilling my coffee, I settled down and quickly found the email from Zoey. After I read it, I printed a copy.

Police responded to a break-in and possible burglary at 2410 West Branch Road. The homeowner indicated that an antique trunk had been opened and parts of it disassembled. A stack of bedding was moved but not stolen. A single old English coin was found in the bottom of the trunk, indicating that it may have contained others. The owners are certain the coin was not there prior to this event. Police are investigating.

Zoey had written that the home was that of Edward Jeffers, whose wife, Constance Haddon Jeffers, had received the trunk as a family heirloom from the Haddon family. The family always thought it was empty. Now it looked like it had a secret compartment! And there might have been some eighteenth-century English coins in it! Much more exciting than the police report seemed to indicate, that's for sure.

Okay, it was time to research. I called Diane.

"They were looking for something!"

"Who is this?" My friend, the comedienne, replied.

"Cute. Now listen." I explained what Zoey had just provided and my analysis. "If this Haddon ancestor hid stuff in the trunk, she might well have hidden things in her clothing too!"

"Wow! That sort of totally makes sense. So then we're saying someone—"

"The Quilt Ripper."

"Yeah, sure, the Quilt Ripper, tore Judy's skirt apart because she, for the sake of argument we will assume this is a female, thought there might still be something hidden in it?"

"I don't know what, maybe coins or jewels?"

"After all these years?"

"I know it seems unlikely. But don't forget, the Haddon Jeffers in Massachusetts thought they just had an old trunk, too. They had no idea there was something valuable hidden in it."

She sighed. "Okay, going farther out on this limb before we saw the tree down behind us, what do you want to do next?"

"We'll do an Internet search on the Haddon family! That's what those ancestry sites are for, right?" I added, "I haven't watched every Sherlock Holmes ever made for nothing." Then I finished with a dramatic flair of my own, lowering my voice and wiggling my eyebrows for my own amusement. "I know his methods."

"I think you might be spending too much time with Queenie." She laughed. "But this is kind of exciting, in an unfortunate way. Okay, I'll come over after dinner and we'll do this."

As I went through my usual day-off routine of laundry, housekeeping, and a bit of grocery shopping, I went from being psyched to sad.

If there had been a treasure in Judy's skirt, the Quilt Ripper had it now. We'd never able to prove a thing and the Smythin's family inheritance was gone. They'd never even know what it was. By the time Diane arrived, I was totally bummed.

She knocked and then stepped right into the kitchen like she always does, Harry growled at her.

"Harry Hathaway. You go lay down!" I spoke sharply and he gave me one of those "I'm not afraid of you" looks before he walked slowly away, tail held high in the air.

"Sorry, Dee Dee."

She had taken a step back but now came all the way in and closed the door. "Geez, he never did that before."

"He disapproves of us trying to figure this thing out," I muttered, feeling like an idiot. "No, I didn't tell him."

She nodded her understanding. "It's uncanny, isn't it? How they know what you're thinking or about to do almost before you do? I can be sitting there watching TV and just thinking about having some ice cream and Snapper will walk straight to the freezer!" She giggled.

"Okay, let's get to it."

We settled into my office/sewing room just off the kitchen with the mandatory glasses of white wine, of course. I have a laptop that I carry back and forth to work, but I prefer the desktop at home. The printer's right next to it, too, just in case we need to print something. We started working our way back through time to the Haddon family's early roots in Massachusetts. We moved quickly through to a decade before the Civil War and then it was slower going.

"Finally!" I said when I found the right period. "So we're looking for a Haddon who came over before the Revolution."

She nodded. A few more clicks. "Here we go. Henry Haddon. Look, Miranda, he lived in Boston between 1758 and 1761 but then moved to Lancaster, Pennsylvania, and died in 1785. That's gotta be our guy."

"We're almost there. I feel it. Now, did he have a wife or sister who came with him?"

Diane, who had taken over the mouse while I refilled our wine glasses and brought in some munchies, peered at the screen. "Got it, wife, Hannah. Aw, nuts." She took the wine glass from my hand. "She went down with the ship, the *Ajax*, August 1759." She took a sip and then gasped. "She was only twenty-four. Lord have mercy!"

She clicked her way through a listing of passenger ships and found it. "It floundered in strong winds just off the coast.

141

They were only a few miles away from land. I know it was long before our time but it still makes me sad."

I sipped and munched and thought out loud. "Well, that's not good. Her baggage should have gone down with her." We sat in thoughtful silence except for the munching of popcorn. "Let's go with the facts and just the facts. The trunk made it; Hannah, may she rest, didn't."

Diane slowly and thoughtfully suggested, "Well, her husband was already here. What if she packed a trunk of stuff for him to bring with him? Maybe clothing and bedding for him and a few pieces of clothing for her? You know, the way we pack an extra outfit in our carry-on in case they lose our luggage, but in reverse."

"Okay. So, for whatever reason," I put it together as I went, "she didn't tell anyone about what she'd hidden! She wanted to, I don't know, maybe surprise her husband when she arrived?"

Diane's face lit up. "Okay, I like it. Women are so devious." As we finished our wine, she added one last thought. "Or maybe some of her stuff washed ashore and was salvaged? Or what if he remarried and the skirt belonged to his second wife? You know, men didn't stay single long at that time. It was too much work to run a house, same as it is now, actually! And they really needed children to work on the farm or in the family business." She pointed the cursor to the Haddon family tree, and then clicked forward.

"Aha! Henry Haddon married Cynthia Stanton in November 1759. Geez, nice to wait until Hannah was cold, dude!"

I shook my head. "I'll bet there's an interesting story behind that. But, moving on, things being what they were at the time, even if the skirt was Hannah's it was 'waste not, want not,' and if it could be made to fit Cynthia I betcha it wound up in her wardrobe!"

"Unless she was a finicky sort, or Henry never handed over Hannah's trunk to her. And imagine how ticked off the second wife would be if she knew Hannah hid stuff in that trunk and clothing and she never found it!" She made a nasty face.

We continued to trace the Haddon ancestors until we reached the present-day cousins. There were only three female cousins remaining that we could find. They shared a maternal grandmother in Virginia Haddon Wilcox. Virginia and her husband had moved to eastern Pennsylvania to the farm where Judy's parents still lived. Judy and Taylor had married local men and remained.

Constance had met Edward in college and moved to Boston where he started his career in finance. When Virginia died she had left the items to her three granddaughters, Judy, Taylor, and Constance. Now the connection was complete.

"I can't believe this. We've completed the family tree in under two hours. God, I love the Internet!" Diane grinned.

"I know. It would have taken me weeks of research at the library to discover what we did here tonight."

Diane looked at the clock on the computer screen. "I'd better get home. It's late and Mark will wonder what happened to me."

"Thanks for your help. I think we now know what's next, don't we?"

"Yes, we do, Sherlock. But let's sleep on it. And with that profound insight, I'm outta here!"

I walked her to the door and shouted as she reached her car, "Good night, Watson!"

I could hear her giggling as she climbed inside.

Chapter Eighteen

The next day was a workday, so I put the Haddon family issues out of mind at least for a few hours and tried to concentrate on my job. It was unlikely that the Quilt Ripper would attack during the day.

Even though we are a small-town library, there is still a ton of paperwork that must be done. We have a terrific computer program for our recordkeeping but we still have to enter the data into it on a daily basis.

I plowed through the mundane tasks of paying bills and reading emails on autopilot. Then I pulled up the scheduling program and plugged in my employees according to their preferred schedules. Even with only three staffers, we have to adjust for time off and work in the volunteers when they are available. So, as easy as it would seem in that we can have a fairly set schedule, there are always tweaks to be made. And this team worked so well together, I wanted to keep it that way and keep them happy. Not always easy.

I felt that I had accomplished a good bit by the end of the day. I returned home to find Harry waiting by his bowls.

"I made a short stop at the market to grab some chicken for my supper and if you are a very, very good boy, I just might share."

He remained glued to the spot, seemingly unimpressed.

"Okay then, let me go change and I'll be back in a jiffy." I went to my bedroom and put on some comfortable yoga pants and yet another old Marine Corps t-shirt.

After giving Harry his kibble and fresh water, I pulled the rotisserie chicken apart and made myself a small salad to go with it. I dropped a few small pieces of the chicken into the bowl and Harry pushed it aside.

"What's up with that? You love chicken. Don't tell me you're upset because I was a little late. Or because Diane and I were researching?" Hands on hips, I read him the riot act. "You are getting to be a spoiled brat lately. Get over yourself, buster!"

I picked up my plate and took it to the living room where I placed it on the tray and turned on the TV. *Two can play this game.* I ate and watched the news.

It was some time later that Harry strutted in and jumped up into his chair. He stood for a minute and looked directly at me. "*Eeow.*"

I gave him my "thinking about it" look, and then relented. "Okay, you're forgiven."

After I'd cleaned up the kitchen and put my dishes in the dishwasher, I picked up Harry's bowls to rinse and every bit of chicken was gone.

"Hope you enjoyed it, you old grouch!" I shouted toward the living room where he was now enjoying his after-dinner nap.

I'd settled into my chair and picked up the mystery I was currently reading, while watching *Jeopardy* and *Wheel of Fortune*. I suspect that Harry mostly likes the sound of Alex Trebek's voice, and the clicking of the spinning wheel.

We were about halfway through *Wheel* when there was a sharp rap at my front door.

"Who is it?" I called through the wood, trying to peer through the peephole while standing back to one side. Old habits die hard and all that.

Assorted giggles answered me. Then I heard Queenie's commanding voice. "This is the Cutler Quilting Guild Number One. We've called an emergency meeting."

I opened the door and they flooded in, carrying several pizzas, two liters of soda, and a six-pack of our cheap local beer.

"Uh, hello," I said to anyone who was listening.

"Come on in, Miranda, make yourself at home." Brittany giggled.

They moved through the house to the kitchen.

"Hey, got any paper plates or cups?"

"In that cabinet just behind you."

"Where's your pizza cutter?"

"Drawer to the right of the sink."

I must have been frowning because Queenie put her arm around my shoulders. "We're here to help you, my dear. Stop making that face."

"Do I need help?"

"Of course you do. So we decided to come over and make a plan."

"What if … I'd had company? What if … I hadn't been alone?"

A sudden silence fell over the group. Diane had come in through the kitchen door in time to hear my comment. She broke the silence by chortling, that's the only word for it. Soon the giggling was deafening.

When she could breathe, Queenie punched me in the arm. "You're such a kidder!" She shook her head and went into the living room.

Five minutes later, she called the group to order by clinking on her soda glass, and welcomed Diane as a guest. Brittany, Diane, and Judy took the sofa. Sarah and Harriet were on the loveseat. Gabe was noticeable by his absence. Queenie had ensconced herself in my chair so I took Harry's recliner. *Full house.* Harry had disappeared, I'm assuming to nap on my bed.

146

And then Taylor and Jake Perryman walked in. I was no longer surprised by anything so I calmly stood up and went to get more chairs from the dining room. But Jake stopped me.

"No need, Miranda. I'm not staying." He looked at his wife.

"I'd like to stay," she said quietly.

So I grabbed a chair and placed it behind her. We all waited for Jake to speak.

He wiped his forehead with the ever-present red handkerchief. "Um, I was asked to come here, Miranda, to verify that alibis have been corroborated for every person in this room for the evening of the break-in at Judy's house. Each one provided a statement that was checked out by a member of the Cutler Police Department, and I can assure you that none of them, or you, are suspects."

He looked at his wife, who smiled and touched his arm before taking her seat. He nodded at me briskly, face red as a beet, and left quickly, closing the door firmly behind him.

Queenie looked at my shocked face. "Miranda, you might want to close your mouth, my dear. That is not a good look for you."

The giggles erupted again. When they finally settled down, Queenie began.

"The matter before the Guild this evening is …," she paused dramatically of course, "… the presence of a thief in our town, or as some are calling this person, the Quilt Ripper."

I looked at Judy, who blushed. "We're not dense, you know." She glared at me.

"Of course not," I muttered in self-defense.

"Right," Queenie continued. "So we've figured out that our calendar may have triggered someone into looking at the heirloom pieces of clothing that were featured, specifically those belonging to Judy and Taylor. Since Judy's skirt has already been … attacked, we figure maybe Taylor's bed jacket will be next. And the only thing stopping the Ripper from doing that already is Jake being the chief of police."

My eyes widened in surprise. "I agree and that's as far as I've gotten, too."

She nodded. "So the logical thing to do is surveillance."

"What?" I gasped. "What?"

Taylor spoke in her soft voice. "Miranda, Jake is planning to come to Pittsburgh with me this weekend. My brother," she stopped and swallowed, "is worse and we need to make … final … arrangements."

"I'm so sorry," I said and a murmur of sympathy made its way around the room.

Judy took over for her. "So we have all agreed that we will watch the house while they're gone. It's doubtful that the Ripper will try anything in the daytime. We'll start our surveillance when it gets dark, say around ten or so, and take two-hour shifts so no one is totally sleep-deprived. What do you think?"

I realized my mouth was hanging open again and closed it before venturing, "Does, uh, Jake know about this?"

Taylor smiled. "Not officially."

Diane chimed in. "What's he gonna charge us with anyway? Illegally looking at a house? We're not planning on breaking and entering, ya know. Joann Roberts, next door, is willing to let us use her spare room that faces the Perryman's house so we can watch in comfort. She has a flea market in Philadelphia anyway. So we're all set."

"And what are you, I mean, we, planning to do if the Ripper shows up?"

There was dead silence for a moment. Then Queenie regained control. "We'll call the cops, obviously. Ron Mitchell and Joe Traxler work weekends, everybody knows that. We'll all put the number on speed dial."

"This person doesn't actually seem dangerous, you know. She or he, because we really don't know which it is, hasn't tried to hurt anyone. Speaking of he ..." I looked around at the group. "Where's Gabe?"

It was a few seconds before Diane spoke up. "I hope you won't be upset, Miranda, we all know you like him and vice versa. But we don't know him. He's still, well, a suspect. He's only been here a few weeks." She waved a hand around the group. "Everyone here is connected to this place. We all know each other or at least each other's families. I'm sorry but we didn't feel safe including him, just in case."

"Does that mean that Jake didn't ask him for an alibi?"

Taylor spoke. "He said he was home in bed, alone."

"Ah." I couldn't help but feel the slight on his behalf. "Well, so was I."

Queenie cleared her throat in dramatic fashion. "Moving on," she said firmly. "Who wants the first shift, ten to midnight?"

Harriet, the older of the twins by three minutes, spoke up. "Wait, we forgot the tricky part. The paper will be running a small story tomorrow announcing that Judy and Taylor will be donating their vintage pieces to a museum in Philadelphia."

Sarah quietly added, "Next week!" They nodded proudly in unison.

"Wow, so it's now or never for the Quilt Ripper to get at Taylor's bed jacket."

Queenie smiled a Cheshire cat smile. "Exactly!"

I couldn't help but smile back. "You girls are awesome." I shrugged. "Okay, I'll take the two to four a.m. shift, that's probably the worst for those of you with kids."

Diane volunteered, "I'll come with you. Since it's not a school night, I don't have to get up early."

Brittany spoke up. "I'm sorry I can't help. My husband's on the night shift at the factory. I've got to stay with the kiddles."

Queenie and Judy took the ten to midnight shift; Sarah and Harriet took midnight to two.

Diane spoke up. "Well, I think we've got this covered, ladies!"

For no reason I can think of, a round of applause broke out.

Meanwhile, the Quilt Ripper was back. She'd checked into a different motel this time, although it didn't appear that anyone was hot on her trail. She couldn't stop smiling and she spent an unreasonable amount of time jingling the pouches of coins.

She'd had dinner at the Appletree Restaurant attached to the motel and picked up the local weekly paper. As she watched the news on TV, she thumbed through it, paying attention to the local tidbits. Suddenly, she sat up straight. *Oh, crap!*

Two local women, Judy Smythin and Taylor Perryman, have announced that they will be donating historic family heirlooms for a textiles exhibit at the Philadelphia Museum of Arts. Mrs. Smythin will be sending a green trapunto skirt, circa 1759, and Mrs. Perryman, a blue bed jacket, circa 1756. Both pieces belong to the Haddon family, who emigrated from England to the Boston

area before the American Revolution. Mrs. Smythin said, "We have been keeping these pieces to ourselves too long. We are delighted to be able to share our legacy with the public." A representative of the Museum will be transporting the items next week. The exhibit will be open to the public in January.

So she had three days to get it done.

She shrugged. *Fine.* Then she'd be on her way to some place warm and wonderful and no one would be the wiser. Maybe she'd even send Aunt Patricia a postcard or two. Probably not.

The next morning, she made her way to the diner for breakfast and listened attentively to the chatter around her.

When she walked in, she spotted a policeman on a cellphone in one of the booths. She slid in behind him.

"I know, honey, I'm sorry. I was really looking forward to seeing your sister and her kids this weekend, but I have to work. Jake's going out to Pittsburgh with his wife. That brother of hers who's sick took a turn for the worse and they need to make some final arrangements."

He listened in silence for a moment.

"Yah, I agree. It's really sad. He's not much older than us and has had cancer for a couple of years. Every time they thought they had it all, more would show up and now, I guess, it's near the end."

Again, he appeared to be listening.

"I know it sucks, but when you look at what Jake and Taylor are going through, I guess it won't hurt me to work a few extra hours."

Silence.

"Yah, Joe and I are gonna split up the hours so I might be able to get home at some point, unless there's any trouble."

The Quilt Ripper smiled as she paid the check. Man, it's a wonder someone doesn't hit the bank in this town like every other week. What a bunch of pushovers, she thought as she walked to her car.

As soon as she was out the door, Sylvia, with a small thrill, picked up the phone.

"Hey, you told me to call if I saw that girl in the photograph. Well, she just left the diner. Yes, I'm positive. She was here a couple of weeks ago, too, then I didn't see her around last week, but she's definitely back. She's wearing a black wig and sunglasses, but it's her." She listened for a moment. "Sure, no problem!"

Gabe thought for a moment. Black hair and sunglasses. He'd seen that girl in the diner a couple of times. She'd been right under their noses for weeks.

"Now we have you," he muttered to himself.

Suddenly, it hit him. Andy had been trying to tell them for weeks. "Stranger in town. Up to no good." Gabe slapped himself upside the head.

God, he wanted this to be over. He'd ruined his chances with Miranda because of this stupid kid. His face softened as he thought about her, all eyes and soft hair, smart and sassy. She made him feel, well, something he hadn't felt for a while. He had to believe she'd give him another chance, even if he was terribly out of practice with women. She had to. He was tired of being alone, but more tired of women coming on too strong, bad first dates, lies, and trying too hard. He wasn't going to give up on her without a fight.

Chapter Nineteen

Friday was a fairly quiet day at the library. I went to the breakroom for coffee about ten and was surprised but pleased to see Andy sitting at the table with a donut and a cup of coffee.

"Hey, Andy! Good morning. How are you? Great! Well, gotta get back to work. See ya later."

He looked up from his book and smiled at me. It caught me off guard. Then I smiled back, almost welling up. It was the first time he had met my eyes and smiled. So I'm a sap, sue me.

When I got on the computer to check my email, I found a note from Queenie cancelling the weekly Quilt Guild meeting for tomorrow afternoon without much of an explanation, something about having to do an inventory for insurance purposes. I assumed that was primarily for Gabe's benefit.

I understood how the other women felt but I still felt guilty leaving him out. Even if he had sort of hurt my feelings and even if I hadn't heard from him since our first and only official date, he didn't seem like a thief, or even a ripper, to me. And he had worked for the government. Although he hadn't gone into details, I'm assuming he would have had significant background checks done before getting that job. Maybe I should have argued harder.

I stopped for Chinese takeout on the way home from work. As Harry and I settled in for the news, me with moo shu chicken and an iced tea, and he digesting his tuna with a water chaser, my phone rang.

I had never been this popular. Phone calls, guests, geez. I sort of missed my old routine of peace and quiet. I looked at Harry and he looked disgusted, too. When I saw who it was, I almost didn't pick up. Okay, I didn't pick up. It went to voice mail.

We watched the news and were settling in for *Jeopardy*, when the phone rang again. And again, I didn't answer. Then I decided to be a sport and check the messages. First, Gabe was asking if he could come over to the house and speak with me. Then he said he was outside and could see the lights and hear the TV. *Oh, nuts!* I'm gonna have to get those black-out drapes and lower the volume on the TV.

I looked at Harry. "What do you think, Harry? Should I call him back or let him stand out there?"

Harry lifted his head, turned and looked at me with narrowed eyes, then lowered it and closed his eyes tightly.

"Oh sure, for someone who always has an opinion, you're not much help when I need one." I walked over to the window and pulled back a corner of the drapery. A dark figure lounged against a car on the street under the streetlight. He waved. I dropped the drape.

"Oh, shit!"

Again, I broke my no-swearing policy. I don't swear much. It just seems, well, uncouth, for a librarian who should be able to use her words, as we say to small children.

I went to the front door, switched on the porchlight, then stepped outside.

He came to me. "Hey."

I nodded. "Hello."

Silence ensued. Awkward, sure, but she who speaks first loses. Everybody knows that. I waited him out.

He cleared his throat. "Might I come in for a minute? I won't stay long, I promise." He held up a cake box. "I brought this in case you hadn't had dessert."

I recognized the box: Randy's Cheesecake, the best in the world, or at least in Pennsylvania, as far as I know. And I eat a lot of cheesecake. I sighed. There was probably no polite way to grab the box, nip back inside, and slam the door, right?

"Sure, come on in."

He smiled ever so slightly, and, holding the cheesecake in front of him like a shield, stepped inside. I went to the kitchen to make coffee and he followed. I don't care what time it is, you must have coffee with cheesecake.

"How are you?" he ventured quietly.

"Fine. And you?" I can do banality as well as the next.

He chuckled. "That pretty much uses up my supply of small talk."

It felt like he was putting it on me to keep this conversation going and I wasn't having any of that. "*You* called and *you* stood out in front of my house until I invited you in. I'm afraid the onus of maintaining the conversation falls squarely on you," I said a bit snappily. Cheesecake only gets you so far.

"You're right." He paused for a moment. "I need to ask you something."

"I'm listening." I cut the cheesecake and put two slices on plates, and then poured two cups of coffee. "Milk or sugar?"

"No, black is fine. Can we sit down?"

"Sure." I plopped not too gracefully into a chair at the kitchen table. "Take a load off."

He sat down and watched while I shoveled a bite of cheesecake into my mouth. I may have closed my eyes for a second. I started to feel better. He took a few bites and a sip of coffee. When I looked up, those blue eyes were boring into me.

"Quilt Guild was cancelled for tomorrow."

I nodded and shrugged. "It happens."

"It hasn't happened since I've been here."

"I guess we were on a roll then. It gets cancelled for lots of reasons. We like it to be a pleasure rather than an obligation."

"You're not going to make this easy, are you?"

I put down my fork, took a sip of hot coffee, slightly burning my tongue, which dulled the good mood that the sugar rush had encouraged, and said sternly, "I have no idea what you're talking about. Or why you're here for that matter."

"Miranda, I'm sorry if I hurt your feelings."

"And yet you didn't rush over here for that, did you? So why are you here?"

"Okay. There's something going on. I feel like everyone else in the guild is involved except me."

I hesitated, which pretty much gave the game away. I really need to practice lying.

"If there is something going on, I need to know."

"I bet you do."

My tone caused him to respond in kind. "And what does that mean?"

"It means that, for all we know, you could be the Quilt Ripper."

He thought about that for a minute. "Well, I'm not."

"You don't have an alibi for the time of the break-in at Judy's."

I met his eyes squarely. And for a moment I was mesmerized by their crystal blue color, but just for a moment, until they crinkled in amusement.

"Do you?"

"*What?*"

"Do you have an alibi?"

I stewed. "I'm not the Ripper."

He leaned toward me. "Neither am I."

I sighed and pushed my plate away. "You're just going to have to chalk it up to being a newcomer here. We've all known each other forever and there's a price to be paid for being the new kid in town."

"So you're all up to something and you're not going to let me help."

I stood. "Sorry, no can do."

He stood. "Okay. But I have to ask you this, Miranda. Please don't do anything that will get anyone hurt. It's just not worth it."

"I don't intend to."

"No one ever does. I'll see myself out." When he moved to the door, I followed.

At the door, he turned and looked down at me sadly. I didn't look him in the eyes; I would have weakened. I stood my ground. He raised his hands as if to touch me, and then dropped them. I took a step back.

"Would it help if I said I think you're quite lovely and it's not you, it's me?"

"No. Not much."

I closed the door. I did not offer him his cheesecake back. I ate another piece and froze the rest. You never know when you might have a cheesecake emergency. But even with extra cheesecake on hand, I still felt off, unhappy, and sort of choked up. *Damn it.*

Chapter Twenty

We all wore black. We hadn't discussed it but we ended up dressed like burglars. I don't know why, exactly, as we were merely watching the house, but it seemed appropriate.

Diane and I had volunteered for the two to four shift, which was the worst, out of deference to the older and the younger. I had no one at home and she said Mark and Ethan would be snoring away and wouldn't even know she was gone.

She picked me up and we parked on the street behind the Perryman's house. We walked through the neighbor's backyard. Diane knocked softly three times (the secret code) and the door opened.

Sarah smiled and whispered, "All quiet."

We followed her upstairs to the guest room where Harriet stood with her binoculars raised. That seemed like overkill to me but I was probably just put out because I hadn't thought to bring mine.

Harriet turned to us with big eyes blooming behind her thick glasses. "There's someone in there," she whispered loudly. "I just saw a light."

We all froze. Now what?

Diane snapped out of it first. "Are you really sure, Harriet?" she whispered back.

The woman nodded.

"Okay." I took a breath. "I've got this." I dialed the number I had programmed in earlier. "Ron? Hi, this is Miranda. Sorry to wake you. Yes, I know I'm whispering.

There's someone in Jake's house. Right." I clicked off. "He'll pick up Joe and be right over."

Diane snapped, "Well, we can't wait. How long will it take to rip the jacket to pieces? We have to go."

Harriet reached into her tote bag and whipped out an object that looked like big, black hand gun.

I was the only one who gasped. "What the heck is that?"

"It's a Taser."

"Are you serious? Do you know how to use that?" Diane asked, obviously impressed.

"I read the directions. Easy-peasy." She smiled, her teeth gleaming too brightly in the dusky room.

We all looked at each other and nodded. Please note that at this point, "hero-type" music should play in the background in the made-for-TV movie of our escapades.

We moved stealthily as one, one squad of chubby, out-of-shape, middle-aged (and some, plus) women, across the yard.

The front door of the Perryman's house was open ever so slightly; the alarm panel was dark. We tiptoed in and stopped to gain our bearings. As we expected, faint noises came from Taylor's home office just down the hall off the kitchen, which also contained her sewing machine and storage. *Oh no, ripping noises.*

Harriet clicked the Taser. The noises stopped. Diane raced down the hall and pushed open the door. A woman in black froze for a moment and then grabbed the bed jacket and ran for the door, knocking Diane and me over and barreling into Sarah. Harriet fired the Taser and it caught Sarah in the middle of the back.

"*Ackkkkk.*" Sarah went down like a shot.

Even the Ripper turned to look before she tore off toward the open door. I spun around and went in pursuit.

Suddenly, a man appeared in the hallway and flew past me toward the Ripper. He'd come in through the back door and he caught her by the ankle, but she twisted loose and sprinted out the door.

The police car was at the curb. Ron and Joe opened the doors, weapons drawn. "STOP! POLICE!" Ron shouted, but the Ripper jumped over the shrubs and took off running down the side street.

Everything stopped for a second, and then Ron and Joe jumped back into the car, hit the siren, and took off in hot pursuit. Figuring they had this, I went over to the man who also wore black. He was on the floor, slumped against the wall, breathing hard.

"Damn it!" he muttered.

I recognized the voice even before someone thought to turn on the lights. "Gabe!"

We didn't have time for questions; Sarah had been pole axed by the Taser and Harriet was crying as she cradled her in her arms.

"Diane, call 911!" I yelled.

"Already did," she answered while trying to comfort Harriet.

Gabe's eyes had followed mine. "What the hell?"

I sighed. "Taser!"

"She'll be okay then." He added, louder, for Harriet's benefit, "She'll be okay. It takes a little while to wear off."

"Ohmigod!"

He looked at me. "No, really, she will."

I grinned wickedly. "It's not that. The Ripper took the jacket." Diane and I exchanged high fives. "But we'll get it back."

"Damn straight we will," Diane declared. I pulled out my cellphone and clicked on the app installed by the security company earlier in the day. "There's a GPS chip in it."

"What?"

I held up the phone to show him the map and wiggled my eyebrows. "Impressive, huh?"

"Jesus, Mary, and Joseph!" He hoisted himself up from the floor and grabbed my hand. "Let's go!"

I looked back at Diane but she waved me on and shrugged a little, indicating she would stay with the twins.

While he drove, I fiddled with the little screen and followed the bouncing ball, so to speak, the way that Howard of Steele Security had shown me.

"Left." We turned. "Right." We turned.

After we had gone through most of Cutler and gone an exit or two on the Interstate, I stopped us.

"She's going to the Drop Inn off Exit 211!"

Gabe smiled grimly. "Right back to her motel. Nice."

"Well, she hardly thinks we'd be following her, does she?" I said slyly.

He thought about it for a moment and then gave it up. "That was brilliant."

"Thank you." I said modestly while thinking, *I know.*

"So tell me."

I settled in comfortably. "I thought about it this morning. Well, yesterday morning now. What was the worst case scenario here where no one was likely to get hurt?"

I paused. "Of course I didn't know then that Harriet would have a Taser." I continued. "Diane and I decided that if we startled the Ripper, she would take the jacket and run."

"Which she did."

"Exactly. So I called Howard down at Steele Security. We went to school together," I added in an aside, "and he said he

161

had a chip we could sew in and follow with a phone app. I went down and got it, we went to the house, sewed it into a corner of the jacket, and there you have it, or as the British say, Bob's your uncle!"

He laughed. "You're a bit of an Anglophile as well as an amateur sleuth, aren't you?"

"Yes to both, I'm afraid. But it seems to be working for us so far."

We were now in the parking lot of the Drop Inn. I glanced over at him. "Okay then, I tracked her and now the ball is in your court." I pointed to the hotel. "She's right there. So how about telling me who you really are and why you're here? And the truth would be nice, for a change."

He rubbed his hands over his face. "Okay. I told you I had worked for the government. That part was true. I was with the FBI for 25 years and then retired to start my own private investigation firm in Boston. About six weeks ago, I got a call from Patricia Moriarty."

"Seriously? Patricia Moriarty, the author?"

"Of course you'd know who she is, wouldn't you? You probably have all of her books at the library."

"That would be a 'yes'."

"Well, her niece ran off and took some research papers she was using for her new novel. They had uncovered the fact that women who were transporting valuables across the Atlantic often arrived to find their trunks broken open and valuables missing. Some of them came up with the idea to hide their jewelry by sewing it into their clothing. It's quite ingenious, really."

"Or hide coins in streamer trunks."

"I'm impressed. How did you know about that?"

"Because she already hit the Haddon home in Massachusetts and found coins in the trunk." I added cattily, "Oh, didn't you know?"

He shook his head but didn't bite back at my remark. "So the bottom line is that I was hired by Patricia to find her niece and bring her home as quietly as possible."

"If I don't seem all that surprised, it's because Zoey spotted Patricia in a restaurant where we were having dinner when she was here. Patricia appeared to be having a serious discussion with a local newspaper reporter. And she was wearing a large hat and dark glasses in the restaurant, which you might want to tell her only makes her presence more obvious in a town the size of Cutler." I added, "Since nothing much happens here, it seemed logical that she'd be involved. We have a noted textile expert in Cutler and an incident involving an antique skirt. Duh!

"Just for my own information, are you really divorced, and do you really have a son, or was that all part of your deception? Is your name really even Gabe Downing?"

He sighed. "All true, Miranda, I never wanted to lie to you. I just had to be discreet and get this job done. I have to admit that for a while there I couldn't wait to get back to Boston, but lately I've been thinking of staying around for a while."

I felt him watching for my reaction. I believed this was the truth.

To my surprise, he leaned over the console and kissed me on the lips, softly and gently. Maybe because I was just a little drowsy at that moment, it took me a few seconds to respond. But it was a good kiss. And by good, I mean I felt heat go through me and my toes curled.

He pulled away, "Let's get this done." He touched my cheek. "So we can get back to the important stuff."

I cleared my throat and blinked. "I take it we don't have a plan?" I looked at my watch. It was pushing three. "So, listen, how's about we go home and … get some sleep?"

He looked at me, puzzled.

"She's probably sleeping herself by now, or tearing the jacket apart, then going to sleep. I doubt she's going to pack and run in the middle of the night."

"This is not the way it's supposed to be done."

"Unless you have a SWAT team waiting around the corner somewhere, we seem to be on our own. And she's already gotten away from us. She's younger and … spryer."

He chuckled. "You don't pull any punches, do you?" He paused then said, ironically, "Just so you know, I've been in touch with Jake and he's aware of why I'm in Cutler."

"Well, I think we lost the deputies." I looked in the side mirror. "Probably just as well. I'd be willing to bet they'd be blasting the sirens coming in. They don't get that many chances so they do that."

He nodded and pulled out his cellphone and dialed the motel. After a little pull and push with the desk clerk, he had her room number. Then he dialed the police station. The deputies had given up their hot pursuit and returned to base. They were on their way home to bed, in other words. Ron answered in a grumpy voice; I could hear him.

"Listen, this is Gabe Downing. The Chief filled you in. I need some surveillance at the Drop Inn off, um, Interstate 80 …"

"Exit 211," I murmured.

"Exit 211. There's a female suspect who's staying there in Room 244. Her name is Amy Moriarty, 21 years old, blonde hair and blue eyes, about 5'6". I just need someone to sit on her until tomorrow morning so I can pick her up." There were a few seconds of listening.

"Okay, good. I'll be back at the motel by nine to relieve you. Thanks for your cooperation."

I made a circling noise with my hands. He nodded.

"Oh, and, please, no sirens Come in quiet and keep it on the down low. Okay, good."

He turned to me with relief in his tired eyes. "I think you're in the wrong career."

I yawned. "Uh-huh." Then I added, "It's not as exciting as it is in the movies, but then again, in the movies, no one ever sleeps."

"Well, it's not that I don't trust your deputies but I'll be back here by eight anyway." He grinned.

"Smart. You can wake up Joe when you get here. But the Ripper, I mean, Amy, is probably gonna get her beauty sleep and not surface until ten or eleven anyway." I shrugged. "Let's face it. Her work here is done."

It took some getting used to, the Quilt Ripper's real name being Amy. It wasn't nearly diabolical enough to be taken seriously.

On the way home, I pushed out a text to my friends: *Ripper tucked in. Pick up morning. Update then. Get some sleep.*

We pulled up in front of my house shortly before four. As I started to get out of the car, Gabe said, "Get some sleep, Miranda. You were a tremendous help tonight. I would have lost her without you."

There was a lot I wanted to say, but at this point I knew it would only be incoherent mumbling, so I got out of the car, closed the door, and walked away.

Harry met me at the door and complained about the lateness of the hour, or rather the earliness of the hour.

I waved him off. "Oh, please, you've already had five or six hours of sleep. Don't even pretend you've been waiting up. Give it a rest."

And so we did.

Chapter Twenty-One

My phone rang and I looked at the clock: 9:30. Darn. It had probably gone down without me. The Quilt Ripper, Amy, I mean, likely didn't need as much beauty sleep as me.

"Hello?"

"I woke you, didn't I? Sorry about that. But I thought you might want to be in on the big wrap-up."

I sat straight up. "You didn't … nab her yet?"

He cleared his throat. "No, I thought I'd wait for you."

"I'm on my way." I threw back the covers. "And, uh, thanks."

"Take your time. There's no sign of movement yet."

I clicked off and raced for the bathroom. Twenty minutes later, I pulled into the lot and dashed into the lobby, breathing hard.

"I'm glad you're here," a deep voice said from my right. I spun around. "She called down to the desk. She's checking out."

"Oh." I looked around. "So where's the SWAT team?"

He looked tired. "I sent the deputy home. I think we can handle this without reinforcements. There is someone else coming though." He angled his head toward the small coffee bar. "Wanna cup?"

"Love one."

Once we had both inhaled some caffeine, he cleared his throat. "Patricia Moriarty will be joining us."

I swallowed my surprise. "Okay. And then you'll arrest Amy?"

"Miranda," he said gently. "Let's talk about this for a minute. Amy took her aunt's notes and quickly realized that the first family had put their articles in a museum where she couldn't get to them. She moved on to the second family, who had simply lost track of their pieces through the generations. All they were able to provide was some correspondence and a diary confirming that the practice existed. The Haddons were the last ones on the list. Our goal has always been to stop her, return whatever property she has taken, get the notes back to Patricia, and keep this whole thing out of the news if we can."

"Okay, so that's why *you* came to town. You learned that Judy and Taylor had inherited items from the Haddon family?"

"Exactly, and who would have ever guessed that my ex-wife's quilting machine would play such a big part in my search. I was able to talk to people in town, and eventually join the Quilt Guild and that's where I learned about the calendar. I did know that Judy and Taylor were descendants of the Haddon family. And, of course, we both know what happened to the third piece, the actual trunk." He gave me a rueful smile.

"So you infiltrated the guild in order to get insider information."

"Something like that. Judy was a member and there was the calendar. As you can tell, by doing the families in order, Amy's not much of a criminal mastermind. I almost had her at Judy's house the first time. But she's young and fast, as we found out."

He thought for a moment and then continued. "About Patricia ... she has, as you might expect, taken this very personally. She's raised Amy since she was eleven when her parents were killed in a car crash. Although she won't ever show it, she's deeply upset, but she also can't afford to allow this scandal to ruin her reputation and credibility."

"Yeah, I guess I get that." I shrugged. "No SWAT team, huh?"

"No SWAT team."

At that moment, the doors swooshed open and the woman herself strutted through in a black suit and red hat, heels, and sunglasses.

"Quickly, one last thing," Gabe said quietly. "Just because the woman has a certain … professional integrity, doesn't mean she's a nice person."

Patricia lowered her sunglasses. "Why in the name of God is SHE here?"

Gabe squared his shoulders. "Because she's the one who thought to put a tracking chip in the bed jacket, therefore, she's the reason we're here and know that Amy is inside."

"*Hmmph.* At least we finally have someone with a modicum of intelligence involved in this case." She glared at Miranda, and if that was meant to be a compliment it didn't sound like one.

Gabe turned to Miranda, "Miranda Hathaway, this is Patricia Moriarty. Patricia, this is Miranda Hathaway."

"Fine, fine. Pleasure. Let's just get this done so I can get the hell out of here." She turned on her heels. "Now I'm going to go and grab that little brat. Is anyone coming with me?"

I tugged on Gabe's sleeve. "Are you sure we shouldn't call the police?"

He loosened my grip and opened his jacket slightly so I could see the shoulder harness and gun under his arm. "We have to prove that there's been a crime first." He patted my hand before he let it go. "I think we've got this, don't you?"

I nodded with more conviction than I felt.

We approached the front desk and Gabe quickly showed the clerk an ID. He asked for directions to Room 244. The somewhat dismayed clerk mumbled something about guest privacy. Gabe leaned over the desk and spoke, but I couldn't hear what he said. Whatever it was, it did the trick.

"Room 244 is out of the elevator and to the left, sir."

Gabe smiled. "Your cooperation will be duly noted."

As we got into the elevator, I turned to him. "Will it?"

"Pardon me?"

"Will his cooperation be duly noted?"

"You're priceless, you know that?" He chuckled.

Dr. Moriarty almost cracked a smile although she tried to hide it.

We all stopped in front of the door, side by side, and looked at each other. Gabe stepped up and pounded.

"Amy Moriarty, this is … the police. Open the door."

The door didn't open right away, and when it did, a slender blonde girl stood there, hair disheveled, with her blue eyes filling quickly. She would have been shaking in her shoes but she wasn't wearing any. She was in her bare feet, wearing boxer shorts and a t-shirt, with her hands in the air. Not at all what I expected!

Patricia stormed past Gabe and gave the girl a good slap, leaving a red mark on her cheek. "You ungrateful little twit. You will never work again, you hear me? After you get out of prison, that is."

Our hardened criminal, known as the notorious Quilt Ripper, burst into tears.

I saw Taylor's torn jacket on the bed. Gabe had stepped between the two women and was speaking to the sobbing girl and trying to keep Patricia away from her. I walked over to the bed and picked up the bed jacket, which was lying next to a black wig.

"Miranda, that's evidence," Gabe reprimanded me quietly.

"But look!" I held up a diamond bracelet. "Ohmigod!"

While I might have hoped that the Ripper had found something, holding it in my hands made it real for the first time. My friends, Judy and Taylor, had an inheritance after all—one that would make a difference in their lives. We, I mean Gabe, confiscated the two pouches of coins from the trunk; the diamond bracelet and a gold ring from Taylor's bed jacket; and a magnificent rope of pearls and a pair of sapphire earrings from Judy's skirt. The pieces were of considerable value in their own right, but even more so because of their age and provenance. Amy, subdued and resigned, confirmed to whom each item belonged.

Once the valuables were recovered and Dr. Moriarty got her notes back, calmer heads began to prevail.

We waited until Amy had gone into the bathroom and dressed. When she returned, Gabe suggested we all get some breakfast and discuss the situation.

We walked to the restaurant next door and found a quiet table in the back. After we had placed our orders and coffee had been delivered, Gabe began.

"Patricia, now that you've calmed down and you have your notes back, I'd like you take a breath and think about what you have gained here. When you write your book, you are going to have a more amazing ending than you could ever have imagined.

"This has bestseller written all over it: research assistant uncovers treasures missing for two centuries hidden in antique textiles and an old trunk!"

He paused for effect in a way that would have done Queenie proud. "You've just gone from a book on historic textiles that a few people would be interested in, to the kind of bestseller Dan Brown made out of *The Da Vinci Code!*"

She glared at him but he could see the wheels had started to turn. So he turned to the Quilt Ripper.

"Amy, what you did was wrong."

The girl's face fell. "I know. I was just so damned tired of being the poor relative; who does all the grunt work for nothing. I do all the research and she writes a bestseller and makes millions from it. It's just not fair."

Patricia attacked again but this time, verbally. "Why you ungrateful little snot! I took you in! I gave you a home!"

"I *know*. You never let me forget it! You didn't even tell me about my trust fund! If I hadn't gotten a letter from that attorney, I would never have known!" The girl's frustration and anger were close to boiling over.

Her aunt's face went to stone. "If it weren't for me you'd have been placed in foster care. I put you through college. I gave you a job."

"Ohmigod, Aunt Patricia, please tell these people the truth. My tuition payments were made from the trust fund. The trust officer at the bank showed me a report of every cent disbursed from my trust account over the years."

Gabe interrupted, "Okay, okay. It's clear that you two have a lot to work out. But we need to deal with the situation at hand."

He nodded sympathetically. "Amy, the way I see it, there are two ways to go here. Let's say that your aunt doesn't press charges for the theft of her research papers."

Patricia opened her mouth to speak, but he stopped her with a raised hand. "Just a minute, Patricia."

"She might take you back to Boston or …"

Amy looked up at him with curiosity and just a tinge of hope in her eyes.

"You can enter an internship program at the FBI."

Her eyes widened. "You would ... they would ... Ohmigod. I could get in, even now?"

He answered seriously. "Well, you've shown a natural curiosity and some good, let's say, investigative skills, which we don't need to identify as breaking and entering. If I put in a good word for you, and ...," he shot another look at Patricia ... "if your aunt and the Haddon family can be convinced not to press charges, I think we could make better use of your talents for the good guys."

For the first time, Amy's face sported a huge smile, and she jumped up and threw her arms around his neck. He gave her a moment and then dislodged her and nudged her back to her seat.

"Oh, Aunt Patricia, puleeezz? Won't you be glad to have me out of your way? This is my big chance!" Amy pleaded.

"Wow, I didn't see that one coming. I'd have to think about it for a while," Patricia started. She continued, grudgingly, "I might need your help to get this book finished." She was clearly thinking about how this would impact her soon-to-be-written bestselling book. "But, if you're willing to come back and help me until it's done, we can look into this intern thing."

Patricia turned to Gabe. "I hope you know what you're letting the FBI in for."

This time Amy jumped up and ran around the table to bear hug her aunt, who gently patted her arm and then pushed her away.

Chapter Twenty-Two

I'd watched in silence. While I found it hard to see Amy get off scot-free after all she had done, it appeared to be a good solution all around.

It would have been hard to find enough evidence to convict her of much in the long run. Nothing could truly be proven to have been stolen, other than the bed jacket. And, as for the research notes, she had done all the work and prepared the notes herself, so what she'd stolen was her own work.

And the truth is that the Haddon cousins would never have known about the treasures, or come into a small fortune, without Amy's research and recovery. I felt pretty sure that the smooth-talking Gabe would find a way to make the Haddon cousins rejoice in their good fortune rather than dwell on how it had come to be in their hands.

After Patricia and Amy drove away, Gabe walked me to my car. I was thinking that my Quilt Guild friends would be dying to hear what had happened.

As if he'd read my mind, Gabe said, "Miranda, why don't you see if the Quilt Guild could hold an emergency meeting at your house? Would you mind? That way we can fill them all in at once."

"I was just thinking about that. It would be easier to tell the story once, wouldn't it?" I pulled out my cell and made the calls, including Diane, of course.

As I pulled my car into the garage and closed the door, Gabe pulled in behind me. We walked through the kitchen door together. Everyone seemed to have made it to my house in record time.

After we had all taken seats, Gabe patiently explained the entire situation, including that he was a retired FBI agent turned private investigator.

There were some exclamations and chatter as this information sank in, but Gabe continued.

"Thank you for the kindness you have all shown to a stranger in your community. Even though I came here for a job, you have all made me feel welcome." He looked at me and I may have blushed slightly as I lowered my eyes.

"Now back to the facts, I was hired by Patricia Moriarty to find her niece."

"Wait, the author, Dr. Patricia Moriarty?" Diane inquired.

"Yes, exactly. Dr. Moriarty is an author and also an expert on antique textiles. She and her niece, Amy, were working on the research for her next book, when they discovered that families who came from England in the 1700s often hid their valuables in clothing or household items to make sure that they weren't pilfered during the long trip.

"Amy and Patricia discovered that some very resourceful women had taken to placing valuables inside the lining of clothing to ensure that it wouldn't be stolen. One particular letter that they found was written by Hannah Haddon. Hannah was the first wife of Henry Haddon. Unfortunately, Hannah's ship was destroyed in a storm off the coast of Massachusetts only miles from its end destination."

Diane nodded and winked at me.

"Oh no!" Judy exclaimed. "She would have been my …" She thought about it. "Great-great-great grandmother!"

"No, actually she wasn't. Henry and Hannah had no children. But the thing is that Hannah must have sent her trunk on to him on an earlier ship, because clearly these items made it over. Our research shows that after Hannah died, Henry married Cynthia Stanton.

"Cynthia was, in fact, your great-great-great grandmother. She and Henry would have utilized the items in the trunk to set up their household and the clothing items would have gone to Cynthia. It seems they never knew about Hannah's secret. And, obviously, no one has had a clue since either."

"This is just unbelievable," Queenie interjected. "That these heirlooms could have been passed down for generations and no one ever realized they held hidden treasures."

"It is unbelievable, but now tell us the rest!" Brittany was impatient, as usual. After everyone glared at her, she added a quiet, "Please!" to the end of her statement.

"Patricia agreed with you that it was unbelievable and told Amy to forget it. So Amy decided to find the treasures to prove her point. She ran off with the research notes and that's when Patricia contacted me."

"So let me get this straight," Harriet began. "The person behind all of this intrigue is a young girl?"

"She's twenty-one," Gabe stated.

"So a twenty-one-year-old is responsible for all of this, and is the notorious …"

"… Quilt Ripper!" Sarah finished.

"Exactly. She's just a kid trying to impress her aunt and to exert her independence." Gabe put a generous spin on the fact that Amy had intended to sell the items and leave the country to escape her domineering Aunt Patricia.

"That brings us up to last night and how, I might add, Miranda and Diane had ingeniously, placed a tracking device in the bed jacket so that we could follow Amy. I'm assuming that you've filled in Brittany up to that point."

"Yes, yes, they did," Brittany spoke up. "But what happened when you nabbed her?"

Queenie just shook her head silently; there was no way they would ever succeed in calming this girl down.

Gabe continued. "We followed her, using the tracking chip, to a motel out on the Interstate and determined that she had settled down for the night, so we went home to get some sleep."

At that statement, Diane's eyes widened and her brows may have flown up practically to her hairline. She stared at me silently, asking the question on everyone's minds.

I stared her down, saying, "It was almost four when Gabe dropped me off at my house. He went to his place to get some sleep, but he had called Joe and Ron to keep an eye on the motel until morning."

Gabe grinned at my need to correct their assumption, and I realized he certainly wouldn't have!

"Right, so I went back out in the morning to relieve Joe who was on watch duty. I called Miranda to see if she wanted to join me for the 'nab' as Brittany so aptly put it."

"And of course, you all know me, I raced out there as fast as I could." That brought a laugh from everyone and many nods of affirmation.

"Okay, Sherlock, then what happened?" Diane asked.

"I'd rather let Gabe tell it. I was just a bystander at this point."

"Right, but if it weren't for you and Diane, we'd never have caught up with her, so you deserved to be there."

Gabe reached over and squeezed my hand, in front of everyone!

"As soon as Patricia arrived—"

"Wait! Patricia Moriarty was here in Cutler and nobody told me?" Diane interrupted.

"Yes, she had been for several days. She didn't want anyone to know because she was here on personal business. No publicity. It wasn't a book tour!" I commented.

"Right, okay, so then the three of us went to the motel room and found a frightened young girl who was in way over her head. She was overwhelmed that she had, in fact, found treasures, both in the trapunto skirt and jacket that belonged to Judy and Taylor and in the trunk the items traveled in, in a house outside of Boston."

He pulled the strand of pearls and the sapphire earrings from his jacket pocket and walked over to Judy, placing them in her hands.

Judy was in tears and could only repeat, "Oh my god, oh my god!" Her hands were shaking.

From his other pocket, he produced the diamond bracelet and gold ring. He placed them in my hands and I showed them to everyone, explaining that these were found in Taylor's bed jacket. We couldn't wait for her to come back from her sad trip to see them.

Gabe then told them about the pouches of English coins that had been taken from a trunk that belonged to Judy's cousin in Allenville, a suburb of Boston. He explained that he would be delivering them in person, when he returned home to Boston.

Many of us were choked up by the time he finished speaking and Judy continued to cry silently. It was simply overwhelming. He gave us a few minutes.

"This entire situation is unbelievable. These wonderful things went undetected for 200 years!" Leave it to Queenie to dramatically summarize for us.

After a few minutes of silence, Brittany, who made up for the twins when it came to contributing to any conversations, spoke up, "Do any of you have any idea how much these jewels are worth? My dad is a jeweler and I helped at the store while I was in school. All together these pieces might be worth hundreds of thousands of dollars."

"Brittany, are you sure?" I ventured, now feeling very nervous about the jewelry in my hands.

Gabe spoke up. "Judy, if Brittany is correct, and I think she might be, maybe we should put all these in a safe place until you and Taylor decide what you want to do with them."

"I agree," I said. "First, let's take photos of everything so Brittany can take them to her dad to get an initial estimate of value, and we'll put all the items in a safe deposit box. Let's do it right away. I'll call Walter at the bank."

I left the room and came back in a few minutes. "He said he'd meet us there in about a half hour. He understood the urgency of getting these items under lock and key."

I continued. "Judy, do you and Tom have a safe deposit box?"

She chuckled nervously. "No. We don't. We never owned anything of value, at least not until now."

"Well, I have a box and if you trust me, I'll put them in mine. Let me go get my key."

Judy agreed and I gave her one of my two keys, just as a show of good faith because she'd still need me with her to access the box. Unless she took a shotgun to it, like old Rafe! That thought tickled me, for some reason.

Everyone got up to leave and Gabe spoke again. "I think we should put the coins in there also, if you don't mind, Miranda. It might be good to keep all the treasures together for now."

"Sure. Absolutely."

"And I'd feel much better if you'd let me drive you and Judy down to the bank."

"Good! Great idea! Are you ready, Judy?"

We printed photos of all the jewels and the coins for each of the cousins while we were at the bank. And Judy said she'd drop off a set to Brittany on her way home. She could hardly wait until Taylor and Jake got back to tell them the entire story.

We were pretty sure that the deputies had already reported to Jake on what an important part they'd played in the apprehension of the dangerous fugitive. This was more excitement than either Joe or Ron had ever had as members of the Cutler Police Department. Or, for sure, would ever have again.

Gabe contacted the Haddon Jeffers family and told them the whole story. He promised to deliver the photographs to their home when he returned to Boston. They agreed to let the coins stay in the safe deposit box for the time being.

When he dropped me off later, he gently said, "I don't know about you, Miranda, but I'm gonna go get some rest. This was quite a day!"

"Yes, it was. Thanks, Gabe, for everything." I walked to the door and went inside.

My quiet home was a relief after all the excitement. The girls had put all the chairs away and everything was back to normal. Harry met me at the door and, for once, wrapped himself around my legs a time or two.

"Thanks, Harry," I whispered, suddenly more than just a little tired. I reached down to scratch his head, "It's definitely been a day."

Chapter Twenty-Three

The rest of the afternoon passed in a blur of trying to process all that had happened in the last twenty-four hours. I might have dozed off in my chair a bit. Harry let me know when it was dinnertime. I dragged myself out to the kitchen and opened cans for both of us—his being cat food and mine being vegetable soup. I stared at the news for a while and then gave it up and went to bed.

But when my head hit the pillow, I was suddenly wide awake. I grabbed the novel I was reading from my nightstand and lost myself in medieval times for a while. I put the book down and realized I had thought about everything except Gabe.

He would no doubt go home to Boston now. His work here was done. He might already be gone. And what did it matter? It wasn't any of my business, really.

But I knew my beautiful, intelligent daughter was right. I should be open to a relationship. I'm only 52, after all, and have a lot of years ahead of me. And I really don't like being alone as much as I've been pretending I do. I do have Harry but it's not the same as having a person to talk to.

Maybe I'll be one of those women who invite another woman to move in with her as a companion and housemate. That would eliminate the stress of finding a man I could live with for the rest of my life. Women are easier to live with and I don't care who says different.

Don't get me wrong; I loved my Harry. But we were really lucky and I knew it. Lightning rarely strikes twice. My Harry had been quite the cuddle bug, in spite of his hard-core

Marine exterior. He loved to hold hands and snuggle at any opportunity. We'd had an active and mutually satisfying sex life until he died. I missed the sex, of course, but most of all the companionship. We could talk for hours about anything, or were both comfortable with a silent room while he watched TV and I read my latest mystery book.

Maybe if I found someone I liked, I'd just invite him home for sex from time to time; something casual with no strings attached. Okay, who was I kidding? I've never done casual in my life and I probably wouldn't start now.

With these thoughts circling, I fell asleep and dreamed of the love in my medieval story that was pure, perfect, and definitely hot! I dreamt of a knight in shining armor who saved me, the fair maiden, from the ruthless villain. When he bowed before me and removed his helmet, he had short white hair and crystal blue eyes. Freud would have a field day. I know I've said that before, but it's one of my favorite sayings.

The following morning my sanity returned when I woke up and realized that I had to go to work! Thankfully, my hours at the library start at nine so I had time for a shower and a cup of coffee before heading out.

I'd decided to grab an egg sandwich on the way and eat it at my desk. After all, I'm the boss and if I want to eat at my desk, I will. Right?

The normal routine of my job felt almost surreal to me after the admittedly bizarre events of the last few days. As I read through the typical Monday morning dose of emails, either deleting or responding, it was hard to get the rhythm back. But I plodded on.

Just before lunch, a knock sounded at my door. "Come in," I called, as I most always do.

A young man wearing khakis and a plaid sport shirt entered, holding the hand of a small, dark-haired woman with huge brown eyes.

I stood. "Good morning, can I help you?"

He smiled and spoke slowly, as if his throat was rusty. "Everyone here has been so kind but I especially wanted Maria to meet you, Miranda."

I have to admit that I was still confused, until suddenly the "light bulb" moment occurred. Shave and haircut! Clean, fresh clothes! No fatigues or camo!

"Oh my god, Andy!" Tears filled my eyes and I came around the desk and bear hugged him.

"This is Maria." I hugged her, too, and she hugged me back, both of us blinking furiously.

"Thank you so much for taking care of my Andy," she said in a quiet voice. "If it weren't for you and the others in this town who looked out for him these past months, I don't know that I'd ever have gotten my husband back."

I reached for the tissue box on my desk and took a couple before handing it to her.

"We're going home today. I wanted to say goodbye and thank you."

"We've still got a long road ahead but we'll take it together." Maria smiled adoringly at Andy. "Andy will continue to meet with the Army psychiatrist and the doctors on a regular basis but he's made a major breakthrough and we're back on track. And that's due in a large part to the people of this town. I've met Sylvia, who gave us breakfast this morning. And a man named Gabe. He joined us when he stopped in at the diner."

"Oh, I'm so glad!" Actually, I was glad to know Gabe was still in town.

"Well, we've gotta get going. Our parents are all at our house in Philly waiting for us and we have a couple hours of driving ahead." Maria stated.

"Of course, and please keep in touch. I'm just so happy for you both."

After they left, I sat down at my desk and pulled myself together. I made a note to send some books to Andy once I had an address. Herb could probably get it for me.

"Well, well, miracles really do happen!" I remarked out loud.

"I'm sorry, am I interrupting?" Gabe poked his head in as he opened my door.

"No, no, come in. I'm a little in shock that's all. Andy and Maria just walked out of here."

Gabe came in and stood in front of my desk. "I passed them on the stairs. And I agree that's quite a miracle."

"They mentioned that you had breakfast with them this morning."

"Yeah, When I stopped in, Sylvia came out to direct me to a booth at the rear of the diner. She introduced me to that handsome young man and his pretty wife and I have to admit, it took me a minute to realize who it was." He smiled.

"Maria said that when Andy called her yesterday and asked if he could come home, she packed a bag and drove out here immediately. I think they're gonna be okay now."

"I sure hope so."

Now that the Quilt Ripper mystery was solved, all that was left between us was that one actual date and that one pretty great kiss. There was no need to delay the inevitable. His silence was making me uncomfortable. Not good at saying goodbye, I guessed. So I decided to help him get it out and let him get on his way.

"Well? Is there something I can do for you?" I snapped at him, as if he was interrupting my terribly busy day.

"May I sit down?"

"Are you staying that long?" I countered, wittily, I thought.

"Miranda, don't tell me you're still angry with me."

"I'm not angry. Not angry about anything. Why would I be?" I shrugged. "I'm just assuming you came to say goodbye and are on your way back to Boston and your real life. Since your case here is solved, you need to get back to your business."

He cleared his throat. "That's true, but I'd like to explain something. It sounds awfully cliché to say that I haven't dated much since the divorce, even if it's true. So I'll skip to the second part.

"When you're pretending to be someone else, it can get confusing. I was the guy from the Quilt Guild when I asked you to dinner. I, or he, wanted to ask you out, but then I remembered why I was here and that I had a job to do. It isn't fair to start something you're not likely to finish."

He sighed. "I didn't know whether promising a second date that I might not be around for would be worse than just not asking." He shot me a pained look. "Now I think—no, I know—I made the wrong choice."

I was speechless, which, as you know, doesn't happen often. He stood up and came around the desk. He put a hand on each of my arms and pulled me to my feet. Then he bent down and kissed me, softly at first, but then a little more passionately. I put my arms around his neck and kissed him back, until I realized what I was doing and pulled away.

While I was catching my breath, he grinned at me. "No matter what happens, I owed you that. And I owed me that, too."

Well, damn. There's nothing worse than getting things straightened out in your mind then having someone throw you a curve ball you don't know if you want to catch.

Thankfully, he turned and walked toward the door. But before he reached it, he turned around and walked back within a few feet of me. My heart started to race just at the thought that he might kiss me again, but he didn't.

"If I were to ask you to dinner tonight, say at the Seafood Palace, do you think you might go?" I heard the hesitation in his voice and it surprised me.

I smiled, "You'll just have to ask to find out now, won't you?"

Meet the authors…

Photo by Jackie Rhule

Mary Devlin Lynch and Debbie Devlin Zook are sisters who have been avid readers since childhood. They discovered several years ago that they also share a passion for writing. *The Quilt Ripper* is their first Miranda Hathaway novel.

<u>Other Books by the Devlin Sisters</u>
The Witherspoon Adventures:
    Beautiful Disaster (Magee-Book 1)
    Burnt Roses (Melissa-Book 2) with Beth Devlin-Keune
    Before Everafter (Madison-Book 3)
    Relative Unknown - Sequel
The Cayden Wright Adventure Series:
    The Wright Move, Book 1
    The Wright One, Book 2
    The Wright Woman, Book 3
Meredith Abbott Adventures
    Lying for a Living: Meredith Abbott's
       Adventures in Hollywood (1)
    Dying for a Headline: Meredith Abbott's
       Adventures in England (2)

We will appreciate your reviews on Amazon!

<u>Contact Information:</u>
E-mail: devlinsbooks@gmail.com Facebook: devlinsbooks
Twitter: @devlinsbooks   Blog: www.devlinsbooks.com

CPSIA information can be obtained at www.ICGtesting.com
Printed in the USA
LVOW10s1442260516
490113LV00015B/656/P

9 780692 616611